"Tea Hačić-Vlahović takes pride in turning lowbrow into vision, a party report into Baroque Conceptismo, rats and pigeons into prophets. In short, she is the academy's wet dream: possessing the ability to read the present with jokes, not footnotes."

—*SPIKE ART MAGAZINE*

"Tea Hačić-Vlahović has an uncanny ability to both thrill and terrorize her readers with deadpan humor and electric prose that cut like a knife. Reading *Give Me Danger* feels like stepping inside all the iconic parties you're not invited to, as told by the only girl who can get you in. Our heroine, Val, a writer, endures a barrage of casual degradation and exploitation that exists in the cultural milieu she traffics in; but Val is no victim, she is keenly aware of the transactional nature of modern relationships and plays the cards she's dealt with a biting self-awareness. A phantasmagoric romp through a dystopian present-day Los Angeles, where the decadence of martinis, velvet and room service co-mingle with rats, violence and trash. This book is a shimmering salve for my internet-addled brain; it makes me want to log off, unearth my sluttiest dress, and go out."

—**NADA ALIC, AUTHOR OF** *BAD THOUGHTS*

"Tea Hačić-Vlahović is a peerless writer, unrivalled. Tea's work is highly stylized, playful and voice-y, pop yet literary and always undeniably her own. It's like nothing else being published today. Tea and her work are stand-outs. I will never stop singing their praises."

—ALLIE ROWBOTTOM, AUTHOR OF *JELL-O GIRLS* AND *AESTHETICA*

"Nobody writes compulsive sexy-horror-envy-intimacy like Tea Hačić-Vlahović. This book will make you laugh at the elaborate facades which are possible to conjure in this rotten world, and, often in the same sentence, weep at their inevitable failures. A bonafide zinger, and I don't say that lightly."

—MEGAN NOLAN, AUTHOR OF *ACTS OF DESPERATION*

"*Give Me Danger* is a deliriously sharp, glitter-soaked literary satire about grief, ambition, delusion, and the modern condition of always performing—even in private. It's haunted, hilarious, and heartbreakingly real. If your therapist says 'unpack that,' this book already has. Perfect for fans of destructive women with excellent taste—this novel feels like a breakup text from the universe."

—BRITTANY ACKERMAN, AUTHOR OF *THE BRITTANYS* AND *THE PERPETUAL MOTION MACHINE*

GIVE ME DANGER

CLASH FICTION

Give Me Danger
Copyright © 2025 by Tea Hačić-Vlahović
Cover by Alex Schubert
ISBN: 9781960988829 (paperback)

CLASH Books
Troy, NY
clashbooks.com
Distributed by Consortium
All rights reserved.
First Edition 2025

This is a work of fiction. Unless otherwise indicated, all the names, characters, businesses, places, events, and incidents in this book are either the product of the author's imagination or used in a fictitious manner. Any resemblance to actual persons, living or dead, or actual events is purely coincidental.

No part of this book may be reproduced in any form or by any electronic or mechanical means, including information storage and retrieval systems, without written permission from the author, except for the use of brief quotations in a book review.

GIVE ME DANGER

TEA HAČIĆ-VLAHOVIĆ

For Winkle

*"ONCE IN A WHILE, ONCE IN A WHILE
YOU GOT TO BURN DOWN YOUR HOUSE,
KEEP YOUR DREAMING ALIVE."*

– THE KILLS

CHAPTER 1
DEVIL'S DAUGHTER

"I got revenge on the man who raped me by living his dream. He failed as a writer in Los Angeles, so that's who I became. Vengeance will set you free, but it can take a lifetime to get back at somebody."

"Is that right." The doctor tugged on a glove.

"Mostly, I moved to LA so I'd never have to wear pants again." Val shifted in the chair, crinkling the paper. It stuck to her back, sticky with sweat.

"Have you considered what we discussed last time?" His latex finger poked her eyes.

"Eye bags are part of my heritage; all Balkan women have them." She jerked away.

"Don't be scared," he teased.

"I can't do anything drastic today, I have a flight tomorrow."

"My technique causes minimal bruising." He winked. "Nobody will notice, you'll just look softer, less harsh."

The world is run by men who won't take no for an answer. "I'm off to New York," she stated. "The haggard look reigns supreme."

"What's in New York?" He feigned interest.

"A friend's memorial. Well, more of a mentor than

friend. My publisher. *Would-be* publisher. Leonardo Castello. Have you heard of him?"

The doctor shrugged and she went on, "He's a legend, a visionary, Aquarius, obviously. He was publishing my next novel, which was huge for me. Everything he touched was legit. *New Yorker* magazine shit." A tear leaked from her eye. Syringe in mid-air, the doctor stared. "Anyway, he did a bad batch of heroin and overdosed at the Roxy." *Sure, he isn't a psychologist, but a doctor is a doctor.*

"I'm sorry to hear that." He tried frowning but had limited muscle mobility. The expression he created wasn't one of concern. Excess injections limit people's facial expressions to confusion or shame. "So, no fillers this time. Just your usual."

"Yep." The needle hit and she winced. Pain didn't show itself in her forehead anymore, but pain doesn't disappear. It finds other outlets. Maybe her elbow looked depressed, or her stomach seemed stressed. "Ow." When the poison mixed with her blood, she forced herself to sit still like a kid at the dentist, thinking, *why am I doing this to myself?* The doctor could hit a nerve and leave her face mangled for life, half her mug sagging like some comic book villain.

She used to worry how she'd explain the hypothetical accident to her husband, since she hid her procedures from him. He judged women harshly for their upkeep as well as their lack of effort, expecting women to maintain their unnatural beauty naturally. So, she'd cover the bruises—which lingered twenty-four hours post-injection—with powder. He wouldn't have noticed either way. He had no idea her bitter line—where a third eye should be—was silenced. Replaced by sleek, submissive skin. As poet Rachel Rabbit White said, "It takes a lot of products to look like a product."

"Deep breaths," The Doc advised.

She breathed with relief knowing she'd be frozen

again. Nobody could know her feelings unless she spoke of them.

Closing her eyes, she recalled how a fuckboy once told her that couples struggle because men can't read women's faces. They were in the Bronson Bar bathroom doing blow. She'd met him at Pink Dot, a convenience store on Sunset Boulevard. He rang her up and hooked her with a line. She'd asked how his day was going and he'd replied, "It's just getting started so I'm still in shock." It was four in the afternoon. Anyway, according to him, if a woman had work done, fights were her fault. "I'm pretty sure my husband knows I'm upset when I'm sobbing naked on the floor." She scoffed at him between lines. "And he doesn't care."

"Can I do this off your tits?" the fuckboy asked, lifting her shirt. He licked the coke around her nipples. "I'm talking micro-aggressions and micro-expressions." He gulped the muck that slid down his throat.

"I need to take a shit," she said.

"But I'm so hard." He clenched his sweatpants, bulge in fist.

"You can watch." She shrugged, dropping her jeans.

"Are you joking?" he asked. "I can't tell."

"Almost done," The Doc promised. "The last round is spicy."

"I'm ready." She slipped back into thought.

The fuckboy proved hard to get rid of—he felt she owed him for the blow. A drunk blonde offered her a ride to Tenants of the Trees. They'd only met in the smoking area where the blonde was holding court, telling everyone who would listen about her audition at Jumbo's Clown Room. She'd been classically trained to dance since childhood and only recently learned to shed clothes. Blazing through her pack of cigarettes in the smoking area, she'd been composed, insisting stripping was beneath her. But in the car with Val she screamed through red lights, blacked out. "Those Jumbo's Clown hoes think they're better than me!" It didn't go well, apparently. To think how many bad auditions are to blame for road rage rampages. Val closed her eyes and waited for a crash that never came. The next time she went to Jumbo's Clown Room, the blonde was onstage. Some people get what they deserve.

Blood crept down her cheek. "There goes last night's wine." The Doc thought he was so clever, slathering her head in gel.

"Vodka." She corrected him.

"So that's $700 today. Shall we book the next appointment?" The receptionist peered into her computer screen with CIA-level concentration, fake lashes flapping like butterfly wings. "Let's see...three months from now?"

"Kind of presumptuous to assume I'll be alive then," Val said.

"Excuse me?" She blinked. *Flap, flap.*

"Yeah, why not," Val swiped her card.

"Okay! Have a great day!"

Must be nice to be stupid, Val thought, walking down the hallway. In the mirrored elevator she examined the puncture bumps on her skin. She bruised and bled easily, worse if she drank before appointments. Everyone knew the rules of injections and she was no rookie. But her last drink of the night was usually in the morning. As a reflex she reached for the powder in her purse. Then she remembered her husband wouldn't be there when she got home.

The cars all looked the same, a sea of ugly grays. Val held her key out and clicked it so her ride would yell, "It's me!"

"Oh my God, are you Val Vatra?" A botched-face girl grabbed her arm in the parking lot. Her lopsided cheeks and lips were inflated to cartoonish proportions. Val guessed she was barely thirty though she looked older. Bad work ages worse than tanning without sunscreen. "Can we take a pic?" Her phone was raised like a rock ready to strike a fish.

"My forehead is fucked up."

"I'll edit it."

"I'd rather not." She turned toward the sound of her horn and heard the girl say *bitch* behind her back. Her readers embarrassed her, and she found them annoying. It was no surprise, as her writing was lowbrow. *Malibu Babylon* was more Pulp than Pulitzer. It was her first novel, based on her first marriage.

Caleb.

Engine revving, she watched the parking lot girl get into her Lexus, probably on her way to two kids and a real estate agent. *Malibu Babylon's* GoodReads reviews were posted by housewives. The only press worth noting was in Women's Magazines. Book Clubs pushing her book were run by reality stars. Her BookTokers were addicted to bottle curls and yoga pants. As a feminist she knew this shouldn't bug her, but she couldn't lie to herself. Real literature is read by everyone, meaning men. Books read only by women were less than. Chick lit. Romance peddled at Gelson's Supermarket. The trash made waves from LA to Tokyo but failed to splash New York.

Poor Caleb.

The island's critics formed a circle jerk and went limp, unable to get off on it. Literary elites mocked it on Substack and in Subtweets. Those she longed to impress most made fun of her "melodramatic prose." She cared more about opinions than numbers. Selling copies means nothing if it means losing respect. She didn't want to be a bestselling author, she wanted to be a *serious* writer, of *literature*. Since her humiliating release she avoided New York City. When the film adaptation premiered, she only attended its LA screening.

Soho's Angelika, her favorite theater, played *Malibu,* too. Instead of flying out to see the miracle, she stayed home and wallowed. Pictured her rivals throwing trash at the screen.

Imagined Caleb tossing himself off a building.

Baby still ties his shoes with bunny ears.

She made a small fortune and bought herself a beach house. Life in the hills would only lead to overdosing at Chateau Marmont. So, she slept between the sea and the highway. The ocean scared her if she stared at it too long.

CHAPTER 2
BLUR MOON

Her house was the shape of a brick. Cement, glass and metal. A staircase spiraled in front with steps so steep she feared stepping. The death stairs led from her bedroom to the balcony, which hovered four feet off the sidewalk. Teens flew by on skateboards. On weekends, she shut her windows to keep out the smell of hot dogs.

A homeless kid lived in a sleeping bag on the beach. Sand Boy, she named him. Val watched him sleep from her bed when she couldn't. Insomniacs are meant for foreign countries, with internal clocks set to far hemispheres. His rags revealed a good body. She tried manifesting him breaking in and crawling into bed with her but knew manifesting was bullshit. Tangled in sheets, she knew her disco nap wouldn't happen. You aren't supposed to lay down after Botox appointments, they tell you. What will happen if you do? You aren't supposed to exercise, either. That tip she accepted happily, an excuse to skip Pilates. She was relieved not to have to make small talk in class anymore. Though the reason for that was bleak. She'd met her only friend on the West Side in a glutes session last year. She struggled to retain names, so her friend remained "Venice Girl" in her phone and brain. They forged a friendship of convenience at Pilates

Mondays, Wednesdays and Fridays. After class they'd hit Abbot Kinney, eat Butcher's Daughter and drink Intelligentsia, which gave her the runs. They'd talk about nothing. She didn't mind dull discourse if it meant ditching a drive to Silverlake, where her real friends lived. Not that any of them had anything to say either.

Val got out of bed and headed for the bathroom which housed her wardrobe. Touching the clothes she owned inspired feelings of pride reserved for new mothers. She pulled out a suede YSL jacket she'd only worn once and smelled the sleeve longingly as if it belonged to a lover lost in war. She stood back and admired her collection, sighing.

Venice Girl caught a homeless man hiding in her closet. He broke in Friday night and lurked unseen all weekend, watching her suffer a double-day hangover. As she gulped ominous Erewhon potions and binged true crime TV, he sniffed her panties and stockings. When she opened her closet to dress for Monday Pilates, well…her screams drowned those of the sea lions. Trauma sent her out of town and off the face of the Earth. Val had no more friends on the West Side. She tried hanging with a crypto-rich couple in Marina Del Rey, but all their dinner parties turned into sex parties and she didn't take her clothes off for people with fake money. Val didn't trust any currency you couldn't roll up and snort a line with.

She spread La Mer on her cheeks and watched Sand Boy snoozing. She knew he wasn't a pervert like the guy who spied on Venice Girl. Once you've been passed through bad hands you can sense when a dude's sick in the head. This boy was mad, but not violent. The highlight of her day was passing him on her way to the water. Frozen waves woke her in ways coffee couldn't, and she convinced herself the current killed cellulite. She'd walk calmly into the icy water, pretending she was a model in a high-budget, high-stakes photoshoot, with the whole crew waiting on her, yelling it's the last light, last chance to get the shot. That trick had worked since she was a kid. Dripping past his sleeping bag, she longed to invite him upstairs but feared the rejection. Anyway, she reminded herself, even your idols are disappointing once you meet them.

From her toilet seat she stared at framed graffiti. The artist pictured once scribbled the streets and now he repped brands that use sweatshops. Her walls were heavy with paintings she hated by friends who showed at Frieze. Rich kids who dressed poor and said they "hustled" to get where they were. She was the only successful person she knew who came from absence. Her friends were entitled and their lack of shame shamed her. She wanted waiters, maids and drivers to know she'd been one of them, looking sorry to sit while they stood. Her effort only embarrassed everyone. She refused to accept that nobody cared that she didn't get extra points for her struggle. You can't claim to be better than those you choose to associate with. You can only hang at the top if you don't mention your climb.

Her phone beeped. A text from The Man, that said, "Coming." She flushed, wiped, squeezed on a Blumarine dress and stepped into Prada sandals. The first time she wore designer shoes, patent leather Miu Miu, was like turning on the AC. That's how money feels, your suffocated world becomes air-conditioned. Only after it's on you realize you were sweating. Money frees your mind, numbers in your account mean not having to count calories after an anorexic lifetime. The calculator in your head switches off with a sigh. How easy it is to forget the math that kept her lights on. Money means not having to rush, or run, after buses or bosses. If cash can't buy time, why do rich people have more of it?

"5 min!" she replied, slapped on a wig and fake lashes. She always dressed up for The Man. Caleb sensed she had a thing for him when he'd see her getting ready for pick-ups. She'd swear the excitement was only over what he sold. And besides, she and Caleb usually went out after…she made a point of that, to deter suspicions. Not that anything ever happened between her and The Man. Since when were crushes criminal?

The Man wrote, "Ready," and she ran outside.

A Soho House starlet made the connection. "He rarely takes new clients, even with referrals. He deals to Leo, you know? *Sniff.* Like DiCaprio?" Val begged for the number after she tasted coke so pure it made her soul feel the same.

Val's armpits prickled at the sight of The Man's Mustang, up the block with the engine running. The Man had a boxer's body and a Nigerian accent. Her feelings for him felt insane. She knew nothing about him but what she imagined. Daydreams can be dangerous. She slid into his passenger seat and slammed the door. YSL Opium filled the car and she regretted the last spray, knowing an Aries like him got annoyed easily. His radio played "Moanin'" by Charles Mingus. Another thing that drove her mad was his music taste. Each time she saw him he listened to jazz.

"Lookin' good kid," he said without looking at her. His eyes were on the road as they circled the neighborhood. She set a hundred dollars in his coffee holder, grazing his leg with her hand. He handed her a white envelope and she cradled it between her palms. She ordered blow when she missed him, which was often enough to cause nosebleeds. The obsession had formed the first night she sat next to him. His indifference charmed her, and his glare left an ache. Wanting him was illicit and nothing turned her on like a secret. She jerked off after their meetings just to take the edge off. The stints in his car didn't cut it. She tried extending their chats, but they only lasted the time it took to make three right turns. One time she saw him stand up when she said it was her birthday, and he walked to his trunk to cop a free bag.

His absence from the car seat revealed a pressure pillow, the kind used for backaches and hemorrhoids.

"How's it going?" She twisted the wedding ring around her finger nervously.

She thought, *if only he'd take an unexpected turn.*

"Can't complain." He shrugged.

Screech into some alley,

"You can always complain, if you want to." She pushed the ring toward her knuckle.

Park behind a dumpster and shove her head in his lap...

They first met in the parking lot of the Roosevelt Hotel in Hollywood. The Man handed her that white envelope and hooked her for good. Powder in pocket, she went from the hotel's parking lot to its pool. *Font* magazine was throwing a party there. Thin, tanned, in hot pants and platforms, she did LA cosplay.

At the door she flashed her phone with her name Googled. "I'm supposed to meet the editor here and he must have forgotten to list me." Her lie was obvious, but Clipboard Girl valued effort. Inside, she darted to the bathroom and held the door open, dangling the baggie. "Girls, who wants?" It Girls don't forget free drugs. Next party they'll say *hi!!* hoping for an invite to the can. If you don't have any on you it's alright. The It Girls will feel bad for asking, giving you the upper hand. But you'll have it on you because it would be dumb not to. The It Girls stayed in that toilet with her all night. One said, "I can't snort any, I just got my nose done but I'll rub some on my gums."

Val made two actresses party so hard they both went sober the next day. They posted an Instagram video pledging abstinence for the sake of *community*. It was so lame she unfollowed them on her way home that morning. "I got so drunk my Uber driver got a DUI." She captioned a nude she took on the zebra rug in the *Font* editor's bungalow. By the time she met him she didn't bother asking for work. She knew any editor throwing such lavish parties didn't pay his staff.

"That's funny," The Man said without smiling.

"So, you got a lot more work tonight?" She slipped off her wedding ring and put it under her legs.

"The usual."

God, why won't he look at me? What if I just told him I want him? What if I put my hand on his knee and just left it there? Would he continue driving as if nothing's happening? Would he take my hand and move it to his crotch? Would he punch me?

"See you soon." He stopped at her spot and she stepped out. As he sped off, she waved. Her hand looked strange in the air sans a wedding ring. The gold band rode off in his passenger seat. She'd been meaning to drop it there for weeks and finally got the courage. He didn't notice yet, but he would, and he'd come over to return it, so they'd finally talk without a transaction, or not the usual kind, at least.

"You'll be back," she said, rubbing her naked finger.

CHAPTER 3
KENNETH'S CURSE

Val foraged in her kitchen for something to line her stomach with before a night out. She stopped buying groceries regularly after Caleb moved out. The luxury of being single again is not having to take care of anybody, including yourself. Slamming empty drawers closed, she cursed herself. "I'd kill for a sandwich!" Val made killer sandwiches. The less ingredients the better. Some talents are heightened by scarcity. She lived off sandwiches when she moved to LA, to the Beverly Motor Motel. The spot was affordable since it offered no amenities aside from a vending machine, mini fridge, coffee machine, and pool. Lucky her, it was walking distance from the Trader Joe's by the Grove. Val stocked up on white, sliced bread, the kind you can deform with a fingerprint, and ingredients to smash between it. Breakfast sandwiches had almond butter, fig jelly and bananas. For lunch and dinner, she'd stack kosher pickles between Chao vegan cheese and heirloom tomato slathered in habanero sauce. She used Ninja Turtle paper plates and bamboo utensils. It was a happy moment for her. Usually, people only know "how good they have it" in retrospect. But this was one of those rare exceptions, when she realized she was in the middle of a memory. Like knowing you're dreaming inside of a dream. You can do whatever you want. And what do you want? More pickles, please.

Sometimes she went to Swinger's for a fruit bowl and coffee. She'd gaze at Beverly Boulevard and beg it not to fail her. Johnny Knoxville once sat at a booth across from hers. She didn't fuss over Johnny that day at the diner because only people who don't live in LA do that. She lived in LA the moment she set foot in LAX.

Stealing a copy of *Hollywood Babylon* sealed her destiny. She had spent her twenty-third summer in London sleeping with an artist. The morning of her return flight she saw a black book on his shelf. It pulsed in her hand, so she shoved it in her suitcase and left while he slept. When she landed in JFK, she called him to apologize.

"I was possessed," she explained. "I'll mail it back."

"Nah, keep it."

Val breathed relief into the phone. She didn't want to accept his offer too quick but knew she'd keep the book if it killed him. He went on. "That book is cursed."

"What do you mean?" She wasn't *woo-woo* yet. Back then, the only crystal she knew was crystal meth.

"Kenneth Anger signed it and hexed it or something. All I know is I've had shit luck ever since."

"No way."

"Way." She heard his lighter click over the phone. "Don't worry." He blew smoke. "Bad luck looks good on you."

She wasn't worried. She accepted his charity and laughed off the rest. Her artist friends always used being an artist as an excuse to act crazy. He called himself an Art Shaman, which seemed exotic and grand. Later she met dozens of so-called shamans in the canyons; burners who got burned out on their tech money.

Once she hung up on the artist, she flipped to the title page to see Kenneth's dark scribbles. She couldn't make out what they said but since then, she read the book countless times and brought it to each borough. It became ratty and bent, a cherished possession. All her life she wanted a curse and under Kenneth's spell she flourished. She brought the book to LA but lost it somewhere in the move to her beach house.

CHAPTER 4
JIZZ AND JAZZ

Val gave up on sandwich dreams and settled for potato chips. A small bag of Salt & Vinegar was found by her blindly reaching fingers in a far corner of a top cabinet, thrown in there who knows when, in hopes to deter herself from eating them. "Hah!" Tearing the bag open, she coughed as the potent Salt & Vinegar odor attacked her cocaine-coated nostrils. She crunched the chips and scribbled "GROCERIES" on a napkin, thought for a moment and stopped. Maybe she needed new kitchenware. Could a perfect pan get her excited to fry up some tofu? Lately only cocktail glasses inspired her, and hers were all stolen from bars. If you spend thirty dollars on a martini you may as well slip the glass in your purse.

Freshly engaged, she and Caleb bought props for making a home together. They searched flea markets and thrifted for neglected items with potential. The one-eyed owner of a second-hand store warned them that LA would murder their love. His wife (*that whore*) chased the spotlight so far that he couldn't keep up. The light led her away from him. She left him in the dark thirty years ago. He longed for Reno but stuck around in case she returned. Shaking Caleb's shoulders in his shop, he pled, "This city ruins good girls. If you love her, take her away." Caleb replied, "But she isn't a good girl." They bought a vintage Versace tea set from him and got married in Malibu. She broke all the cups by their honeymoon.

Val opened her cupboards hoping to find a forgotten can of tuna but they only housed her old magazines, publications she wrote columns or covers for. Wasted piles of paper she couldn't part with. She met Caleb in Tribeca when she worked for *GooGoo* magazine, in the basement of an art gallery. She was aiming to climb to the rank of Condé Nasty cunt, with an office, company card and abused assistant. Nobody had a clue those days were numbered as media people were paving a sidewalk that ended in a cliff.

She shared the basement with Billy, a douchebag, and Raymond, a narc. Every night he drank with cops. He said 9/11 radicalized him, whatever that meant. Both were greasy alcoholics who bullied Val relentlessly. They dressed like dorks and smelled like cum socks; why they worked at an art magazine was a mystery. Freelancers chipped in from home, including a "fashion director" who sent in shoots from Berlin. Val foolishly felt special for landing a basement spot. She'd met Ana, the founder, over dinner at Indochine. Lychee martinis seduced her as Ana peddled bullshit. "I grew up at the airport." Ana was Eastern European, like Val, but raised in England. Private school educated with designer street "edge." Sharp collarbones, sharp bob, sharp teeth. Val hoped they'd bond over shared backgrounds but they were too different, wealth is its own country.

Ana said *GooGoo* would become a chicer *BOMB*, a cooler *ArtForum*. She oozed money from an abscess that would scab up. In the early days she was limitless and proved it by flying a baby albino tiger to town so Marina Abramović could hold it on the cover. Photo shoots had no cap, they'd order lunch from Balthazar for the crew. She spent Gatsby money on parties. Their first fashion week together, she threw an event at the Standard, with so many celebs in attendance nobody cared when James Franco showed up. Ana got runway invitations Val accepted on her behalf. She sat the Jeremy Scott and Marc Jacobs shows. *I deserve this,* she thought, watching Paris Hilton pick a wedgie.

It's hard to spot rot in real time, easy to look back and go, *oh*. One day Ana declared print dead. "It kills the environment. We're going completely online." No more covers meant no more cover stars. Photo shoots with Sky Ferreira and Daniel Radcliffe had been the norm. Fine, Val thought, let's glide into the future.

Next NYFW Ana forbid her to sit shows. "Your coverage sucked. You can go to the after-parties but only if I approve your clothes. You dress sloppy, not *GooGoo*." She valued fun over self-respect so she emailed Photo Booth pictures of potential fits. Ana didn't reply to them and didn't attend any shows, either. Val resorted to writing runway reports via recycled news from other sites, sourcing photos from social media. Soon most magazines would operate this way, but at the time it felt criminal. How hypocritical, Val thought, blaming print, then wasting a pile of runway invitations. Empty seats mark the fall of civilization! Ana showed up after fashion month tan and aloof. "Fashion what? I was in Tulum." She said we're going another direction. Hold on, she said. The basement crew ate hushed lunches at their desks and waited for late checks.

The glory was fading and journalism wasn't her thing.

Billy would constantly nag, "WHO, WHAT, WHEN, WHERE."

"WHO can say WHAT and WHEN I should write? WHERE is the art in that?"

Asking nepotism brats PR-approved questions was torture. Transcribing interviews made her cringe. But she had a title on LinkedIn.

After work she'd run across the street to the Tribeca

Grand Hotel, before it became the Roxy. She'd count the minutes to clocking out so she'd have just enough time to catch a jazz band playing underground at The Django. Going from one basement to another, her life was subterranean. Most jazz spots in the city were too kitschy, too touristy or too uptown for her. The best place in town was hands-down Tomi Jazz, a tiny Japanese spot where you could eat noodles and drink Suntory; but you had to email them for a reservation even if you were solo, and she rarely felt like trekking to that neighborhood. Having The Django across from work was some kind of mercy.

Val texted Guido, her lawyer. "Let's meet at Sunset Tower, they've got jazz tonight, by the pool."

"I'm already here," he replied. "Meeting with a producer!"

"Good for you, I don't care." She did another line.

The Django never booked shitty bands and always made her feel better. Jazz stayed true regardless of trends. Jazz wasn't touched by algorithms or press releases. Down there she felt her life had meaning, like she'd die a meaningful death.

Like most jazz clubs, The Django was pricey. She could barely buy drinks but boys were free. One night she picked up the drummer. After his set, Caleb was drenched in sweat and easily swayed. She waited as he packed up his kit and said, *you killed.*

That's all it took. His bandmates witnessed the capture.

That night she took him to Paul's Baby Grand, a sidecar stuck to the Roxy. The cocktail lounge doubled as a nightclub. The décor was deserted island fantasy, with palm wallpaper, velvet booths and bartenders cruising in crisp suits. Photographs weren't permitted but smoking was. You had to be on someone's list or in their pants to get in. Her greatest pleasure was showing a nice boy a night out, taking him to the type of place they'd never get in without her and exposing him to what he'd long for long after. Clout was all she had and she used every drop. She fed him blow in the bathroom and he sucked her tits like a baby.

Her identity was *Free Bitch*. If a boy stuck around long enough, he'd end up here: you cheated on me (him) you aren't my boyfriend (her) we live together (him) so you're my roommate (her) you're a bitch (him) *Free Bitch* (her) (said telepathically). Here's the thing, her birth chart was a straight line, with her sun, rising and moon in Sagittarius. All roads led to chaos and her habits couldn't be helped. But Caleb was rare, and after one night together, he snuck up on her and crept under her skin. By morning she couldn't stand him shutting the bathroom door without her coming in. Love came fast and felt primal, all grunts, scents and survival. He made her feel like a wolf hiding from a storm in a cave. Waking up next to him was like skipping school and not getting caught. His skin was milk and cereal. She wanted to do right by him, which meant squashing her nature.

She was virtuous for a year.

One night she had too many beers with a war journalist and let him finger her on a bar stool. All she could do to forget that mistake was to make more of them. When she cheated on past boyfriends, the crime brought them closer; she loved them harder to balance the guilt. This time the formula didn't hit. She resented Caleb for his goodness.

He didn't cheat, why would he? She gave him all he needed and longed for something he lacked.

Her betrayals isolated her.

She recalled her grandma once warning her, "Women are so afraid of being lonely they find a man and then what? He turns his back to you in bed and you're lonelier than ever."

She was still hungry. A freak of nature, coke increased her appetite. She rummaged through her freezer and found ice cream. The spoon barely dented it, so she lit the bottom with her lighter like a junkie. She missed the soft serve ice cream trucks lining Broadway. Her order was always vanilla with rainbow sprinkles. It was never any good, but eating it on the crowded street while walking felt so quintessential New York, like getting a hot dog must be, though she wouldn't know since she didn't eat meat. While she lived in Manhattan, she tried endlessly to recreate the city fantasy, a mix of New York Dolls and *Sex and the City*, but it never hit.

The truth was, by the time she got there, New York was bullshit. Normcore took over. Corny kids with no edge crowded the bars and Russians bought all but the rats. As Instagram rose, magazines crumbled. *GooGoo* was funded by Ana's dad all along; corruption money funneled so recklessly, he pulled the plug on his daughter, who pulled the rug from under her staff. Val went from editor to staff writer to contributor to freelancer in a fashion week. Milk Studios blacklisted her for writing jokes about streetwear. Brands became ruthless Gods. If you refused to suck up to them, *move over*. Countless girls would do it for free. They could because their rent was paid already. They used magazines as a way into the Boom Boom Room. *I'm a writer* was just a cool line to yell at the DJ. Editors were posers and writers were suckers. *VFILES* was fake, *Interview* went bankrupt, *Paper* was trashy, *Gawker* got sketchy, *Vice* was toxic, only *The Cut* seemed cool but those girls never liked Val.

After a few bites she forced herself to put the ice cream back in the freezer, though she longed to finish the tub. The real fantasy she was living was *Bridget Jones' Diary*, only unlike that story, where Bridget rises in the end, Val was falling. Her career and love life were a sandcastle in the rain. Her only hope of redeeming herself had been squashed just recently.

During the social media fueled downfall of Manhattan Media, an underground press crept from the shadows, seemingly overnight. Its arrival changed rules in the right circles. Rebellious spirit came to kill what gnawed at New York's integrity. Sin Street Books was run by some mysterious renegade. He was rumored to work with a wicked music executive, who financed most of it, but the creative agency belonged to one man only: Leonardo Castello. He held out a hand to those drowning in the festering pile of bullshit. But Val had nothing to offer him, no manuscript yet, just a knack for writing headlines and the ability to meet deadlines with a hangover. So, with nowhere else to turn, she clung desperately to *GooGoo* until they changed her password. Billy found out she'd used her account to meet John Waters. She sold the story to *Dazed*, a UK print that paid fifty cents per word.

"You passed on the *Waters* pitch."

"You can't use our email to get to other magazines."

"If y'all acted like a real magazine I wouldn't have to."

"Good luck finding one that wants you."

She left with her tail between her legs and never told Caleb. For months he thought she was in the Tribeca basement when really, she was café-hopping to ghostwrite copy and trash treatments for D-list celebs. Returning to New York media seemed hopeless. She covertly planned her escape to *Hollywood Babylon*.

Copies of her novel lived in drawers under her sink. She hated looking at the thing. The book radiated the failure of her marriage. Had she not manifested their finale in print would they have stayed together? She had no right to indulge in wondering. She'd already made the choice for them both. Their heartbreak became a Blockbuster and Caleb returned to Brooklyn, where he belonged.

"Stop!" She said out loud, slapping herself in the face. "I will not feel guilty!"

She reminded herself that their relationship ended

once already. If Caleb had stood his ground, the pain would have shrunk dramatically. Devastated by her life in New York, she moved out without telling him. She was a coward, maybe, but he was so withdrawn he didn't even notice the black trash bags holding her things. He dumped her when she called him from the Beverly Motor Motel. One night she was in his bed, and the next, California.

"You're kidding." She knew he'd leave her. "Tell me you're kidding."

Any other response would be humiliating. The dump was a tragic relief. By then her shame had spent her. She needed a way out and this way it was on him.

"You bitch!"

Free Bitch.

She accepted his act of mercy and indulged in the grief. A lost relationship takes the edge off moving. The breakup happened in Cancer season, she mourned him through all of Leo summer and by Virgo she was healed. Libra season he showed up, beaming, "I drove my drums cross-country." What could she say? He was a Taurus, Capricorn rising, Libra moon. Once he set his heart on a mistake even God couldn't stop him.

When everyone in LA is a struggling actor waiting tables, finding a table to wait is harder than landing an audition. Swinger's Diner wouldn't hire Val and neither would Canter's Deli. They seemed to think she was too delicate for the work. "A million girls would kill for this job," she pictured the redhead assistant saying in *The Devil Wears Prada.* Finally, lying on her resume got her the graveyard shift at 101 Coffee Shop. 101 was always open, feeding hustlers and industry types. That street hosted wannabe-European spots like La Poubelle and Oaks Market. The Scientology Celebrity Centre loomed over the block and marked it all in its shadow.

Once, Val posted a photo of a muffin near the building, tagging the Scientology Celebrity Centre location, and the post was removed within minutes. It hadn't been reported, nothing about the photo could be deemed obscene. But clearly someone on the inside didn't want to be associated with pastries.

She and Caleb rented a dingy room up the hill in Beachwood Canyon. It was always cold and smelled like mold. Tree roots grew in the plumbing so flushing shit involved a bucket. A miserable couple owned the house. The first month she and Caleb joked they feared walking in on a murder-suicide. Then they stopped joking. The upstairs energy spilled into theirs.

Caleb hung around the diner during Val's shifts, searching online for gigs. Slouched at the counter with his laptop and hair in his eyes. At first seeing him slumped on a stool would bring her joy, but that soon turned to bother. Just as she could barely stand the sight of him, he got hired by a private school to teach music, via Skype, over a plate of pancakes. From then on, he slept while she served and she wrote while he taught. They never left the neighborhood. Los Angeles was impossible to explore when their home was a labyrinth of tension.

Flesh-eating wildlife confirmed LA a violent place. A family of coyotes courted her after dark. First, she met the one she named Larry, lurking around the dumpsters behind her restaurant. Larry was scruffy, scrawny and handsome. He walked with a gangster limp. Strays could always sniff her out as a source. After she seduced him with scraps, he led her to the others. She gained their trust by committing work-crimes. She smuggled cold waffles and greasy bacon, soft Hawaiian rolls and slimy slices of American cheese. During her shift she'd eye customers' plates, swoop in before they finished and add the loot to her grocery bag full of coyote goodies.

When friends called asking about LA she'd tell them about her crew. Their fur, fleas and fury. Her friends would say "dope" and move on to themselves, like they weren't even listening. Mostly they only called while waiting for the train, to confirm New York was still the fun hell to her boring heaven. She spent more quality time with the coyotes than Caleb. He didn't believe her coyote tales, so she recorded videos of them doing coyote things, and her doing human things with them. He watched with his jaw dropped, more animated than he'd been in months, insisting she post them online. "It's comedy gold!" He swore, and he was right. The degenerate gypsy circus acts went viral. In the videos the coyotes ran the show, Val was their pet. People couldn't get enough, so she made more. *The Hollywood Coyotes* got more love than any work she'd done before.

Larry gave her the idea for her book after a brutal fight with Caleb. They stayed up until dawn hurting each other. Usually they whisper-screamed, to not wake the upstairs couple, but this time they didn't care, nothing mattered. Who worries about manners while surviving a flood? On no sleep and in tears, Caleb went to school. Before he came home, Val went to the diner. Neither apologized or made contact all day, which was a first for them. She never minded saying sorry even when she knew a fight wasn't her fault. If a couple eventually makes up, why not speed up the process?

As a rule, they never went to bed angry, no matter how bad it got. But this time something felt broken. She didn't even crave the dopamine hit of a make-up, how he'd hug her head to his chest so she could only breathe his scent. When they slept after arguing, she imagined their subconscious would talk things over, sort things out for the versions of themselves they had to be while awake.

That dark day she checked her phone hourly, but he still hadn't texted, and each time the realization made her colder, number toward him. A foreign, rotten heart hung in her chest, painting her world black.

Still no word by the time she clocked out and fed

Larry and his crew. With nothing left to do, she stalled, hoping to create a new video, but nothing hit, they weren't inspired. She dropped into a Balkan squat, in a corner by the dumpster and cried, realizing she'd rather sleep in the garbage than near her husband's regret. Larry approached her and she flashed her iPhone screen, blasting off with comments.

"You're famous, Larry."

He snarled at her.

"Am I exploiting you?"

He lifted his leg and pissed. Then he began limping away.

"Don't leave me," she pled.

He turned his yellow eyes toward her and she saw herself reflected.

"Take me with you."

Honesty's the only way out, is what she heard him say as he strutted up the street toward the canyon. That night, Caleb slept alone as she wrote the first pages in the living room, a space rarely used, fearing awkward bump-ins between couples. Often they skipped whole meals to avoid meeting in the kitchen. Thus began her new routine, pounding sugar-free Red Bull all night and writing with Larry in mind. *Malibu Babylon* described the collapse of her marriage before it happened. Prose punctuated by secrets.

Albert Camus said the only way to deal with an unfree world is to become so free that your very existence is an act of rebellion. But he was a man. Was she a brave woman fighting for autonomy? Or was she betraying goodness itself? She couldn't rely on her emotions to guide her because the same source that begged her to stay was the one telling her to run. The radio frequency of her soul changed stations erratically, switching from AM to FM. How can you expect a weather forecast from something like that?

Her heart was a broken compass leading her through

a dark forest, like the one in *Snow White*, where floating eyeballs watched branches tug at her clothes and shred them, while she screamed, losing her mind. The trees and eyes her words. She broke the news to him before a 4.5 earthquake. The planet shook her head, NO. A sign. Don't do it. What's important? Him. What's important? Being loved.

She ignored the Earth; it was now or never. They cried through the aftershocks, shaking with the trash cans on the street. He held her and said I'll protect you, but it was him clinging for life.

CHAPTER 5
SATURN OVER SUNSET

She connected a playlist to her Bluetooth, neglecting the record player and vinyl collection that reminded her of Caleb. Various playlists for varying degrees of self-destructive mood-enhancement. The current, "Pička," or "Cunt," in Croatian, was punk heavy. Prison Affair, Amyl and the Sniffers and her favorite, Iggy Pop. "Search & Destroy" played as she pranced around her kitchen, doing bumps and taking swigs. "This is you, don't forget it!" She mumbled to herself. "You're Iggy Pop, not some dumb bitch." She nodded her head as she rubbed coke on her gums.

Iggy once said, in some interview, that when he left his young wife for the band, he promised himself to make the hurt worthy. He had to ensure whatever he did would be so important that any collateral damage would be a necessary evil, like taxes. He went on to change history. Nobody knows about that girl, and if they do, they're grateful for her sacrifice; had he stayed behind, to be a husband, punk rock would have died before it could live. Iggy Pop living the life of an average human would have held back humanity! Leaving her wasn't just un-wrong, it was right.

Val's writing didn't inspire a cultural movement, and

her film royalties weren't worth two lives. What she killed loomed over her success, as punishment. The pain tainted each paycheck. Now she daydreamed of turning down future offers. Spitting in the face of any producer crass enough to turn her life into their bottom line. The daydreams left her cold and empty. She knew she wouldn't find herself at that table again. So, she had to do something remarkable, to make it make sense.

Be a real writer, go down in history! So, when some kid in the distant future looks her up online, on whatever device they'll use then—a fingernail implant, maybe—he'll see she was married, and his response will be: of course, she had to write that book and of course she had to leave. Since she was young, she wanted to be a writer so she could shape opinions. Real writers rule the world like politicians. Stories break and build society, like war. Literature survives wars. Her writing would save her from hers, but it had to be extraordinary, and *Malibu Babylon* wasn't.

When the film came out, a big-shot agent swooped in and offered hope. But all their meetings were dreadful. He took her to haunted Hollywood spots—Musso and Frank—where dead memories were dumped on the living. She could feel the hands on knees of starlets under tables. Hearts broken, dreams squashed, pussies wrecked. Maybe it was that underlying sense of doom that kept her from trusting. Under his eye she feared she'd become a sculpture. Something grotesque at the Edition Hotel, hanging from the ceiling, crafted to be enjoyed by people who paid others to butter their bread. If her life boiled down to her work, which it did, and her work boiled down to that, which it would, her life would stay sad. She torched that bridge and remained unsigned.

During her rise to hack-fame and fall from so-called grace, she wrote her second novel. She hoped that, if the first one destroyed her love, this one could kill her ego. She built penance that could bring redemption. The kind of religious reward one gets for eating their newborn. The second she typed THE END she took a nervous shit, and then immediately after, DM'd Leonardo. "Can I send you my new manuscript?" He'd passed on *Malibu Babylon*, obviously. "This one's more your style," she promised. She'd deleted all the exclamation points, since he tweeted once that he loathed them. *Malibu Babylon* was dripping in her favorite punctuation. She waited weeks to hear back, torturing herself with thoughts of him making fun of the book in smoky rooms with greater writers. Finally, he DM'd a question. "Have you sent this to anybody else." (He also hated question marks).

"Just you."

"It's *three fire emojis*"

She celebrated the text exchange at Jones Hollywood. "You don't understand. He's mainstream and underground, he's got media respect and street cred. That's impossible in this industry, this industry full of nerds, that's all most editors are these days, they're bitter nerds, because most of them wanted to be writers and couldn't, so they punish real writers by publishing bullshit. And the advances, don't get me started, they give a small percentage of authors enormous advances, and most authors peanuts, making it impossible for them to make a living. Writers walk around feeling like hobbyists. Do you know what that does to one's spirit? It's all about distribution of wealth, as in most industries. But you'd think this one should have some sort of backbone. Isn't this ART? Doesn't it MATTER? And agents, MY GOD. They're just gatekeepers, did you know you can't get published without an agent? It's like real estate, you need a middleman, otherwise good luck. There's self-publishing, which is a death sentence, or maybe you can submit to some tiny indy house that doesn't have distribution. I guess you keep your dignity that way, but what's the point of dignity if nobody knows about it? I'm kidding. But anyway, this guy, the one that likes my novel, he's in charge of Sin Street Books, and they're known for even publishing unsigned authors. He tweeted once that he would only accept un-signed manuscripts! It pissed so many people off, it was incredible. It's cutting-edge stuff most houses are afraid to bet on, and guess what? Everything sells, REALLY SELLS, like big time, one of his authors even won some award, I don't remember which one, but it was a big one. Oh, thank you! That looks fabulous."

"Are you closing or keeping it open?"

"Open. Being published by him will take me from like, literary personality, or whatever, to legitimate author."

The bartender turned to help another drunk, and she smiled to herself as she looked again at Leonardo's message, which was now a screenshot turned into the wallpaper of her iPhone.

How happy she was in that moment, how hopeful. And now she was back to the drawing board, stuck with this schmuck who sucked up to anyone dropping a name off a Hollywood hill.

She slugged the prosecco, rinsed the glass, rubbed coke on her gums and chewed Altoids. Coke breath kills. She tossed keys, cards, cash, lipstick, cigarettes, matches, mirror, mace and drugs into her Versace Palazzo purse, which was martini olive green, like her Challenger Hellcat.

People say New York couples stay together for their apartments, but she knew the truth was transportation, not real estate. Splitting by subway is unpoetic and taxi dumps are pathetic. Nobody wants to make a big scene, grab their things and have to carry them to the L train. Or worse, wait on the street for a Lyft. Abandoning your love is the juiciest moment; you're scared and unhinged, moving forward only because it's too late to turn back. The last thing you need is your man chasing you down

Bedford to gaslight sense into you before your ride shows.

An escape calls for a soundtrack and you can ask your driver to connect your device but he'll never play it loud enough and you won't be able to scream by yourself in the dark of the Pacific Coast Highway.

She pulled up to the Sunset Tower and handed her keys to valet, which was such a waste, but there was no time to park on Fountain, she was already late for drinks with Guido. Only in LA do you end up hanging out with your lawyer.

She'd hired Guido to handle her movie contract because Hollywood types are vampires and if you aren't sharp, they'll suck you dry. She needed a man on her side, but the one she found served her neck on a platter. Guido finessed a contract that allowed cash to crush creativity. The producers hired a corny screenwriter and kept her from having input. All her notes were ignored. The executives said the truest parts of her story weren't believable or relatable. They toned down the reality and turned up the drama. Caleb's character became a villain and hers was a classic victim. The film was cast wrong, scored badly and edited sloppily.

Audiences ate it up and her book took on new life. The ordeal made her lose hair but she still felt she owed Guido, for the million. Her soul money. She sold hers and Caleb's to the industry.

"What's with the wig?" Guido sat at the Sunset Tower Bar wearing gaudy Gucci. Did he buy the clothes with her soul money? Did those square-toed Prada shoes materialize when she kissed strangers? Did Caleb's cries create that Cartier watch?

Guido's posture suggested he was three martinis deep. He was a cocky Italian she would have slept with had he not laid her friends already. They told her he's a sadist but that was no shock, Leos are greedy lovers.

"Oh this?" She patted her matted head. "I dress up for

my dealer." She kissed his cheek and grabbed the stool beside his.

"You're insane." He snapped at the waiter. "Another dirty martini." He turned to her. "You like it dirty." A gleam in his eye. "I'm gonna start pushing your manuscript."

"Not yet."

"Get a grip, girl." He slapped her back. "It's been a week."

"Fuck you, dude." She snarled. The regulars turned. "I'm a mess." She whispered. "I went to NOBU Malibu and couldn't touch my sake. Mike Tyson was there and he seemed scared of me."

"Why are you whispering?"

"I knew Leonardo died before anyone else did, I felt him leave us. I was morbidly depressed that day and I couldn't get out of bed. So I texted him and he didn't reply and I said to myself, *he's gone*. The next morning, I found out, my friend Vanessa told me the news, but I already knew."

"You sound crazy."

"The last picture ever taken of him that night he wore the shirt I sent him, the one with my naked body across the chest, so he died with me on his heart, unable to protect him." She pressed a napkin between her eyelids and blinked. A black puddle bled onto the paper.

"That reminds me, I need your merch for the office."

"Shut up. Ugh, it's all so depressing! Now I've got to grovel with those literary losers. They think they're so great just because they did MFAs and publish zines sold in Dimes Square."

"New York is embarrassing." Guido watched a girl's ass walk through the room in a tight bandage dress.

"Yeah, I'm excited about one thing, though."

"Oh yeah?" He winked at the girl and she made a disgusted face.

"I'll find the dude who sold the bad smack and get revenge."

He turned his attention back to Val and laughed in her face. "You're ridiculous."

She grabbed her bag and rose. "I'm powdering my nose."

"Hold up." Guido rushed after her.

"What are you doing?" She planted herself between him and the bathroom.

"I want a bump."

"This isn't Zebulon."

"What's Zebulon?"

"Are you serious?" She was too tired to argue with a lawyer, much less an Italian. She let him follow her inside. On the way to the stall, she glimpsed herself in the mirror. She didn't know how she looked; it seemed every day someone else stared back.

Guido squeezed in with her and cut lines while she peed. She caught him sneaking a peek at the panties curled between her knees.

"This stuff is great," Guido said, tilting his head back.

"My Guy is the greatest."

"Give me his number."

"No way." She wiped.

"I've asked a million times!"

"I know. You're desperate." She flushed.

"I get it." He jeered.

"Get what?" She pulled up her panties and grabbed his straw.

"Why share your source when people only call you for it."

"Bingo." *Sniff.*

"Better than why people call you."

"Why do they?"

"Because they contractually have to."

Back at the bar, Val found a New York ghost in her seat. Spencer was a compulsive liar and a Gemini. In his heyday he'd opened doors all over Manhattan. Up & Down, Holy Mountain, his Saint Mark's loft. Val was always on his list and his name made it to her blacklist. The details of why she hated him were blurry but surely he'd refresh her memory.

"Spence!" She squealed like a pig. "What are you doing here?"

"Bitch!" Spencer sipped the martini Guido had bought her.

"How are you? I'm blessed. Booked and busy!"

According to Instagram, Spencer was an astrologer to the stars but in reality, he was a househusband in London, having fled NYC after killing his reputation on reality TV.

"Good for you." She rolled her eyes.

"You look great." He raised his brows. "Love the wig."

"And your Prada Uggs." She gagged. "So chic."

Guido was like, "Get a room."

Spencer threw his key card at him.

Guido ordered champagne for the suite and made Val pay for it. He was on apps the whole time and a couple flutes later he left to get laid. Val and Spencer were left to indulge in the sacred ritual: shit talk on blow. Their brains were vessels for gossip and their bodies possessed by dust.

When the lights go on at a club, most people crash or hook up. Cokeheads find an after-party. Not for fun. They're slaves to the demon in their pocket. After hours, addicts scuttle away to worship her, on someone's kitchen counter or living room floor, where she can shine. LA cradles this craze. It's so easy to end up at a mansion. But don't let being poolside fool you. The glamour distracts from your disgrace, the coke uses you. It's all edging with no orgasm, it's raving for twelve hours straight waiting for the bass to drop but knowing it cannot. Black hole bliss! The euphoria is fleeting and followed by darkness. The joy is the anticipation, ordering is the high, or waiting for a trip to the bathroom. Once you're in the stall you can't wait to come back, so you may as well stay locked in all night. Crawl into the toilet. Coke is empty potential, like the fools who do it. "But I only do bumps." And yet you still find yourself desperate. "I don't pay for it." Oh, but you do, and how.

"Call your plug." Spencer stuck his tongue inside the bag, then ripped it apart and sucked on the plastic.

"Not now." She wouldn't call her Man twice in one night, not since she did it once and hated how he looked at her. She dreaded the thought of him thinking her a cokehead, hoping that punctuality, grooming and manners made her seem like a nice girl who was simply invited to *lots* of parties. Sloppily she rose from the coffee table smeared in residue. Her knees popped from being cross-legged on the carpet for hours.

"So." She groaned. "This was fun."

"What are you doing?" He grabbed her arm.

"You aren't going."

She shook him off. "Party over dude."

"I'll order drinks." He reached for the room service menu.

"Spence, I've got a flight tomorrow."

She snatched her shoes.

"Please don't go. You can sleep here."

"I need to pack."

"I'll get you a new flight." He always pulled this shit. "You want business class?" He scrolled through his phone. He'd do anything to avoid his own company. "I found a red-eye for tomorrow night. We can do brunch at the pool." He begged. She flinched. He was so pathetic, it made her feel good about herself.

"Get up," she ordered. "We're going to Chateau."

"For real?"

"One drink."

. . .

Chateau Marmont was down the street from Sunset Tower. They could walk there, which was rare in LA. Everybody loved the Chateau but she loved it differently, she loved its sincerity. It tried so hard to be a French castle. Elites worshipped the estate for its sleazy legacy—celebrities fucking and dying. History worth celebrating. To her the building was the celebrity. Its soft, moldy scent, the creaky walls and dusty carpets. An air of mystery. Stepping inside shifted the vibe, another dimension prowled in those halls.

The Door Lady was an ageless British brunette. She wore dangling diamond earrings and long silk robes, her makeup was a porcelain mask, her scent something bespoke, crafted for her by some Parisian lover. Every time Val saw her, she claimed to be moving back to London, but then she was always there. The Door Lady had been kind to her since day one. Val knew about the hotel from *Hollywood Babylon*, so she showed up one spring night without a reservation or room number, wearing a shearling coat with a bikini underneath. Her East coast brain thought it was the right move. The Door Lady smiled at her effort and hushed her in.

The bikini got her a dinner invite before she could order a drink. A handsome gray-haired man led her to the garden dining room. Uniformed staff twisted between tables to serve the upper class—and those mooching off them. The man put her at his round table. He was the future president's son, said the escort sitting beside her. WeedGirl was her name. She said they were getting serious. He'd splurged on a suite for a month instead of going to rehab. He learned how to cook crack in the room's kitchen. The man invited her to join them upstairs and WeedGirl pinched her leg under the table. Val assured her not to worry, she didn't care for politics.

After Caesar salad and champagne on his tab she left for the smoke room, an outdoor area with benches, covered in curtains, like circus tents. There she met Beck and Billy Corgan and some new rock stars hanging onto them. The young ones dropped a bag of K on the ground which she hid in her shoe. In the bathroom she found a crack pipe in a velvet baggie. Then walked around the piano bar asking, "Does this crack pipe belong to you?" Nobody had the balls to claim it, so she dropped it in an old woman's open Birkin bag in the lobby.

Needing to throw up in style, she knocked on room doors upstairs. Some guy opened up and let her vomit in his WC. She'd read the rooms were dumpy but how bare they were startled her. Its charm was what rich people thought being poor was like, at a thousand or more per night. Before leaving she pocketed a harmonica off his coffee table. The Chateau was magic like that. You'd walk in for cocktails and end up directing an argument with Sorrentino, only to distract everyone from the fact that you're stealing his shades. The place was expensive, but she always earned back what she spent. When men intruded on her nights alone at the bar, she'd make them pay for the burden with a room number for her tab and sex in a suite she'd sometimes regret, but only until after she got tested. She was extremely paranoid about STDs, even when protected, which made her sluttiness feel like an accomplishment, an act of bravery, exposure therapy. The clinic she frequented was on Santa Monica Blvd, in WeHo, so her gyno was a gay guy who didn't judge her promiscuity, just her pussy.

Val and Spencer waltzed to the bar where they spotted a locally famous starlet named Avalon. The Cancer never made it big because she got caught up in an abusive relationship with a man who looked like Rasputin. She was known for her tiny frame and natural red hair. She was also known for being an annoying crack head. She'd show you a potato sack and say, "Do you like my purse? I made it."

If you were dumb enough to offer her drugs, she'd take more than her share. You know the people who do a key bump for each nostril when you only fill your left? Two is already too many. She'd do three or four or more until you pried the bag from her claws. Val was careful not to make fun of Avalon because she suspected people thought of her the same way. Comradery for the obnoxious. That night Avalon's signature red hair was hidden by a brown wig.

"What's on your head?" Val asked.

"I could ask you the same." Avalon grinned. She took a moment to consider being mysterious and decided against it. "I'm incognito. I'm banned from here since last year." She turned and sipped her drink. "What's new with you?" She hiccupped.

Val hated when people pulled this shit. Avalon wouldn't give up her secret without being asked. She wanted to let it hang in the air just to spite her, to say, you aren't that interesting, but as a writer she had to know.

"Why were you banned?"

"I was caught fucking a busboy in a closet."

Bingo. The three of them ended up naked in the swimming pool. Spencer got out and hovered on the edge of the deep end. "Watch this." He peed into the blue like a fountain angel. That was Val's cue. She pulled herself out of the pool, grabbed her clothes and ran to the back door. The staff yelled at the other two as she got dressed on Marmont Lane, body glowing under Netflix billboards. Avalon was smart and kept her wig on in the water.

CHAPTER 6
BLACK TIDE

She couldn't remember driving home but found herself in bed. Sweating through her blanket, she promised her pillow she'd never use again. Heart racing, teeth grinding, spirit drowning in despair, shame saran-wrapped her soul. Coke comedowns were the depths of sorrow, reminders that sadness weighs more than happiness.

With no chance at sleep, she squinted at her phone and refreshed her email. Farfetch informed her they shipped a package, but she couldn't recall what she'd ordered. Life was what happened between one brown box and the next. Some podcast wanted an interview, and an underwear brand begged to collab.

She deleted all the new shit and scrolled down to find the last mail from Leonardo. Each line was memorized. She forwarded it to herself, so it was the first one in her inbox. His name sat on top like a king. Leonardo believed in her work, and nobody would ever know that but her.

The movie of their last call replayed in her head…

"Hey, can you hear me?" Leonardo lives nine hours in the future, in the Italian villa he inherited from his grandfather. His studio is dimly lit and cluttered with art and books. Hunched over Val's printed manuscript, he's wearing a white undershirt and plaid shorts.

"Yeah! Can you see me?" Val sits in her kitchen, hands sweating in her lap, legs bouncing under the table. Her knee knocks the wood and she flinches. Her outfit, a Mugler skirt suit, had been pressed for the occasion.

"Yep. You look like a million bucks." Leonardo rolls a cigarette, sprinkling tobacco on Chapter Three. "How are you?"

"Kind of hungover."

Her headache is laser sharp; she never wakes up this early.

"Same." He laughs, licking the rolling paper.

"What did you get into last night?"

"The usual, went out for one drink and came home with the birds chirping."

"Those damn birds, is there anything worse?"

"There really isn't. I think they're God's messengers, sent specifically to make me feel like shit."

"Hah." He doesn't laugh hard enough to convince Val he doesn't hate her. She digs her fingernails into her wrist.

"I love the book," he says. She releases her nails, leaving tiny red crescent moons. "I just have a few notes."

"Yeah! Whatever you want, I'm open to change. I have no ego when it comes to notes. Just email me whatever and I'll get into it."

"That's not necessary, we can do it now."

"You mean, over Zoom?"

"Yeah, unless you've got somewhere to be."

"I'm totally free." She grins.

"Cool." He lights his cigarette. Special men do simple things stylishly, like Bob Dylan or Pete Doherty. The way Leonardo smokes is art. If only she could write one sentence that made somebody feel the way she felt watching him blow smoke at the screen.

"I don't know if you remember this, but I sent you my

first book and you passed. It happened while I was covering Art Basel Miami for some magazine. The whole week was ruined for me. I didn't even care when I met Courtney Love. I'm not telling you that to make you feel bad, but so you know that working with you means so much to me."

"I remember that. I don't feel bad. You managed without me."

"Technically, sure. But my first book is trashy, in retrospect. Or it was marketed that way. I'm still not sure what happened. But from now on, I want to be taken seriously."

"Why the hell would you want that?"

After that call they talked daily. He told her about his husband and the slow life in Italy—after reigning in New York for years, he moved there permanently to be with his *Amore*. In return she'd complain about LA and offer up any anecdotes that might impress him.

They had a surprising amount in common, like an appreciation for jazz and a love of misunderstood animals. During his time living in Times Square, he grew fond of the rats. "They're smart, they're sneaky, they're running things, but they've got bad PR." He said. "Speaking of, I have a great publicist for your book. Amelia, she's the best in the city. And she's your age. I think she'll like you, but if she doesn't, she'll still rep you because I told her to." Val didn't say she knew who Amelia was or mention that she unfollowed her on Twitter since reading her scathing *Malibu Babylon* review. But none of that would matter with him on her side. He was Capo of the lit mob.

After hanging up she'd be covered in sweat, like a middle-schooler after prank-calling a crush. The adrenaline rush would lead to a crash, and she'd have to take a nap. After his accident she still listened to his old voice memos, watched videos of him playing the piano, with a mirror hanging in front of it, so he could admire himself while improvising. The dead texts taunted her but she couldn't resist revisiting how they'd promised the kind of friendship she didn't deserve.

She gnawed the insides of her cheeks raw while watching Instagram stories. Feeling especially masochistic, she checked Caleb's profile. She'd resist texting him again. She'd surprise him, call from inside the city. He couldn't avoid her then. He knew he needed to sign papers. She couldn't believe he wasn't hers anymore. The pain of checking on him was punishment for her sins. He must know she's looking, want her to, otherwise she'd be blocked. The girls he fucked clogged his feed. Connecticut chicks cosplaying bohemians in Bushwick with overgrown roots and K habits. Basic girls with personalities ruled by algorithms. Birds who followed trends and men with blind abandon. Women who didn't deserve him. She dove into a negative thought spiral.

That's on you, him balls deep in mid pussy. I feel so bad for him, having to hang out with boring bitches. How could he go from me to them? But he always wanted a normal girl, that was the problem. What was special about you is exactly what annoyed him. You could have held on, couldn't you? It wasn't that bad, was it? Now you won't be old together. No more cold walks to the wash and fold, cozy nights on the couch, your head in his lap. Never again will you watch him pour your wine at a restaurant then turn the bottle upside down in the bucket. That's your fault. He'll never wake you up with a latte, even though he knows you drink black coffee, forcing you into extra calories. That smile he made just for you will never be used. He cared about you in a real, adult, Emergency Contact way. Now that love, meant to last, is a memory. You betrayed your favorite person. If you knew someone else hurt him like you did, you'd kill them! You betrayed yourself, too, the best version of you. This will hurt until you die. You ruined the good in your life. Why are the bitches he's fucking so ugly?

She scrolled all the way down to a picture of them together. He didn't archive their pictures, as she had. As if to say, "who cares?" She felt nauseous. Thinking he was sad because of her made her sad, but thinking he wasn't sad because of her made her sadder.

Dawn crept into her bedroom as Sand Boy was stretching out in pink light—her fallen angel. She longed for comfort, feeling especially fragile after finding Caleb's clothes while packing in her comedown. He'd left behind a puffer jacket and corduroy pants from some skateboard brand.

She jerked out of bed, threw on a kimono and clutched his things to her chest. With uneven steps she spiraled down the death stairs. Sand Boy didn't see her pace toward him. People always invaded his space.

"Hey, dude." She startled him.

The tumbleweed sat up and grinned. Sharp bones stretched leathered skin. Tangled hair and black toenails curled upwards. He smelled like yeast and salt. His face was pure beauty, the kind poets fail to describe. He could have been a runway model or a cult leader. A puddle of Cheerios was arranged in the shape of a whale in the sand by his side.

"What's up?" he croaked.

"Sorry to bother you." She wasn't sorry, though, was she?

"It's chill." He cracked his neck.

"I've got some stuff for you, it's barely used." She grinned.

Sand Boy eyed her bundle. "I can't take that." He shook his head.

"Sure, you can."

"Here's the thing." He considered his words. "I'm trying to have less stuff."

She studied his stuff: a hoodie balled into a pillow on the soiled sleeping bag, two plastic water bottles, the puddle of cereal and a backpack.

"Here's the thing," She needed to give him something or have him take something. Her self-esteem depended on it. The same impulse control issue that propelled her into over-sharing secrets with complete strangers at bars, or worse, her nemesis, secrets that should require the other party to sign an NDA before disclosing, pushed her to say the following. "I'm going out of town; would you like to house-sit?"

Gatorade eyes glared. "Huh?"

Commit to the bit. "I live right over there." She pointed over her shoulder.

"I know you do." He raised his eyebrows.

"Well?"

"Uh…" He shifted uneasily.

"This isn't a trap." She assured him.

"Look, you're sweet, but I'll pass." He laid down. "Too much responsibility." He turned his bony back.

She scoffed, stood and waited for a word. He left her on "read" in person. Mortified, she trudged back upstairs and shoved the clothes under her bed. Nobody breaks hearts like a Pisces; she knew this from adolescence. The only boy who ever deserted her had been a green-eyed poet born on March 6th. They were meant to run away together but he left without her.

Back in her room, Sand Boy's absence filled the atmosphere, as if he were meant to be there.

She started a bath and in the tub she tried getting off to him. She had to at least get something out of their interaction. He humiliated her in the sand so maybe he could go further in her head. She pictured him spitting in her face or tying her to a streetlamp, but it was no use, she lost her boner. Getting off was the only way to relieve stress and these days it seemed impossible. She couldn't let go of pretense even by herself.

Washing off last night's makeup, her used lashes swirled toward the drain. She plucked them from the water and placed them on the soap. The wet caterpillars had been through so much she didn't have the heart to trash them. They could house-sit since Sand Boy wouldn't.

She threw on a tracksuit and checked her bags before leaving. Boots, pumps, platforms, day dresses, night dresses, jeans, tights, t-shirts, ugly underwear, hot underwear, biker jacket, fur coat, makeup, tampons, day purse, night purse and a good wig. The one with human hair that cost a fortune. Her laptop, perfume and tarot cards went in the carry-on. The Vans backpack she'd had since she was a virgin. In the back pocket she placed her diary and the papers for Caleb.

She pulled a card for the trip. Reading cards always calmed her. Sometimes they didn't say what you wanted to hear. In that case, you re-shuffle and re-pull. Like telling all of your friends the same story until one finally responds the way you hope. Asking in her head what to expect next week, she pulled the Five of Wands. *Battle, tension and competition with others. Unable to move forward with your goals. Rather than being able to work, you're running up against constant opposition.*

Writers aren't comrades, they're rivals. The memorial would be a catastrophe. Bitchy editors, bloodthirsty authors, catty bookfluencers, snobby agents, cruel journalists, that publicist cunt Amelia and The Man Who XXXXX Her. His birth chart was trash.

CHAPTER 7
SIN STREET

To pass the time in the Uber ride to LAX she Google image searched herself. No doubt blonde her was hotter. Val had ruined her hair to be taken seriously as an author. Bravely, she left Donatella platinum for mousy pixie. When her friends asked why she cut her hair so short she'd say, "So I have something to look forward to." Blonde her was younger.

One picture always made it to the top of the search algorithm, at La Bain, glazed in sweat and dead-eyed, smiling coyly at the flash. In retrospect she found the image lovely. The night it was taken she felt hideous. After the snap she cried in the bathroom about being fat. She wasted her youth worrying about weight. By the time she resigned to her body she was in her thirties, old enough to worry about age. As a kid she obsessively observed girls' legs and checked their thigh gaps.

Now she only saw faces, frown lines, crow's feet, nasolabial folds, sun spots and enlarged pores. She was nine the last time she lived in her body without worrying how it looked. But even then, she recalled flipping through Delia's catalogues and thinking her knees were too knobby.

Getty Images labeled her an influencer because she

had followers. That kind of status was worse than death in her industry. Writers shouldn't be popular, not while they're alive, and they certainly shouldn't be hot. A real writer is disfiguring their spine and going blind over an old typewriter on a crappy desk at some squalid apartment in a forgotten place, like Siberia, ideally. A real writer flirts with death since their health is ignored for the sake of their work.

Art before everything! Writers should be ugly at least and deformed at best. She would resist getting fillers. Under eye bags made her look like she stayed up all night typing. She tweeted, "Disgusting how the Getty family made a fortune from owning images of me."

Airports used to excite her but now they incited violent urges. The terrorists did win, sucking the fun out of travel. Her perfume was too big to carry-on, and the security lady made her throw it away. If only they knew she failed chemistry. Stupid people should be allowed to bring liquids on airplanes. Especially liquids that cost over $100. Val hoped the lady would keep the perfume and think of her when she used it.

While waiting for boarding, she got burnt black coffee and cruised the bookstore. Only dead authors can be taken seriously at Hudson News. *Malibu Babylon* was sold there once, between reality star memoirs and fantasy novels that confirmed her trashy status. Selling out means success you can't relish; you climb by stomping your own reputation. She skipped over the novels and grabbed *Italian Vogue*, the only *Vogue* worth buying, especially since she couldn't read it. She hadn't read a book all year.

On the flight she sat next to a fat man who smelled like whiskey and pressed his knee into hers. When she crossed her right leg over her left, to avoid his, he only spread out more. A woman a few rows ahead was reading *Malibu Babylon*. Val wanted to yell, "Don't bother reading further. It only goes downhill from here."

She downed a Xanax with beer and closed her eyes. She always had nightmares and recently her terrors involved Caleb, rip tides and deadlines. Drooped in her seat, she dreamed she was stranded in a glass box in the ocean. One by one, zombies came out from the water to curse her. She had nowhere to run. Caleb stood by the door, and she yelled at him and screamed for help but he didn't flinch, he just watched the heads bobbing in the waves waiting their turn.

"Ma'am." A flight attendant shook her awake. "You're crying."

"So what?" she grumbled.

"It's disturbing the other passengers."

"Babies cry on airplanes."

"You aren't a baby."

Val knew only freaks get airport food on their way out of the terminal. But a donut upon arrival became a ritual over the years and JFK airport had a Dunkin' Donuts by the taxi line. Aren't traditions what make us human?

She nibbled her treat in the squeaky leather seat. Slowly the skyline rolled into view. The city looked chic from inside the cab but on the streets, chaos rules. Collective nervous energy makes the city a noisy blister, aching to burst. New York is a mindfuck, the dimensions don't make sense. It's too grand and tiny all at once. Break your neck trying to see the skyscraper tops, crawl on your knees toward the last party. If you put a microscope on the streets, you'd find the atoms having a brawl. It's an expanding galaxy, forever growing, toward a black hole.

She'd taken the open space, the sprawling nothing, the dark matter of LA for granted. Los Angeles is a big blanket thrown across a hardwood floor. California skies are mystical. It's no wonder people join cults and buy crystals.

She closed her eyes and inhaled the sweet doughy aroma in her paper bag. Caleb, when caught in a good mood on a night off, would grab six donuts from Mitchell's and drive them to the desert. In a couple speedy hours, you hit the moon. He'd make them a miraculous fire and they'd roast their donuts on sticks. When sugar burnt under stars, she was sure he was her destiny.

"Hey, miss!" the driver snapped. Val opened her eyes and was in Tribeca. She wiped her glazed drool off the door and gathered her things, *sorry*-ing. The wind swirled around and, in a gust, pushed her toward the hotel. Swivel doors propelled her to the check-in counter. The staff was aloof, reminding her to adjust her attitude. Lower expectations, increased pain tolerance. East coast, baby!

The Roxy rooms were the size of Chateau bathrooms. In the time it takes to piss she was slapped by a closet and punched by the sink. She could afford the suite, but Leonardo would have taken a single room, street view. So, she got that too. Exhausted from the trip and her hangover, she stayed up for jazz at The Django. She had never stayed in the hotel before, so reaching the club directly from her room seemed like a dream.

Once showered she changed into black stockings and a bra with a leather jacket.

CLANK! Went the trash bin.

Startled, she turned. The bin tipped over and rolled back and forth on its belly. From its mouth scuttled an iPhone sized black rat with a *Vogue* cigarette tail. The Rat's left ear was chipped like someone had taken a bite out of it. Otherwise, he seemed healthy, with glistening fur and a plump belly.

Upon making eye contact with her he ran under the bed.

"I'll deal with you later," she said, shutting the door.

Heading downstairs, she recalled all the times she saw jazz at that hotel. Past versions of her, distant stars. Her memory dimensions were distorted, like angel dust vision. A TV screen in front of your face feels miles away. She tried reaching backward, to warn herself about something, but couldn't remember what.

"Dirty Chopin." The band began wailing as she got her drink. Everything was as she'd hoped; the host remembered her and got her the front row two top. The crowd was attractive, if typical. Bankers with sugar babies, refined uptown couples, a gang of queens & queers, and nerdy NYU students. The band was a Mingus-inspired orchestra. Not bad but not new. "Too-toot-zap!" Despite appearances, she was not having fun. Addicts up their dosage once bliss wears off. How can you turn up life's volume?

Between songs, the bandleader chatted in an Appalachian drawl. "My girl is madder than a rattlesnake with a loose tooth…" The saying reminded her of home. This pond by her place, in Boone, had ducks in it. Winters it would freeze over, but the ducks couldn't fly south, because someone clipped their wings. They'd just sit on the ice and shiver. "Ain't got enough sense to pour piss out a bucket." He cackled. She bubbled with rage. In that squalidly sober moment, it hit her: in all the years watching jazz there, she'd not once seen a woman on stage.

"Fuck this," she said, leaving a mess of cash on the table.

The bandleader eyed her as she stood from her seat. "Foller your own lights," he called into the mic. Everyone stared as she escaped, poisoned face scowling.

The glare burned her inside and she had to leave.

· · ·

She rushed upstairs back to her room. She fiddled with the room key until she finally got the door open. Seconds later, Val shed her clothes and slid under the covers that were tucked in, which drove her crazy. Who wanted their bedsheets tucked in? Only a psycho would sleep that way, or someone as worn out as her.

Val closed her eyes and imagined herself a mummy. Something moved under the mattress.

"Is that you, perfect little creature?"

The Rat crawled onto the blanket. His claws slowly pawed their way toward her belly. She froze, not from fear. "Come up here, I'll cuddle you."

Unsure at first, he walked up to her chest, and when she didn't protest, he curled into a ball and stayed there. His back rose and fell as she sang him a lullaby. "The Devil to Pay," Johnny Cash's warning to women like her.

They drifted off together.

CHAPTER 8
NOTHING SPICES UP A MARRIAGE LIKE A DIVORCE

> Daily Horoscope: Sagittarius:
> A friend comes looking for answers.
> Don't show your hand.
> You're building a house for your secrets.

No hangover greeted her that morning but still she took pills with her coffee. In a perfect reality she'd spend her trip lounging in the room or walking aimlessly, but too many people had to be seen before the memorial.

The Rat zigzagged between her feet as she got ready.

"Be careful or I'll stomp you." She picked him up and held him at eye-level. "You've got something...I can't put my finger on it." He sneezed and sprayed her cheek. "Yes, that's it," she wiped her face, "dignified elegance." He waved his tail. "What are you doing here, huh? Don't you have a gutter to run to?" The Rat licked his paws and slicked back his ears. "That's me, always projecting. You're welcome to stay, of course. Just don't get caught. They'll make you pay. Work in the kitchen."

She placed him on her pillow. There he stared at her, solemnly, as if he must say something useful, like, it's raining later bring an umbrella. But she left before he could.

Once she was out the door he tried snuggling on the cushion, switching spots, with his tail between his arms, then legs, then behind him. His own body felt foreign. He was restless in every position. Only his mood felt familiar. A mixture of boredom and anxiety. He needed a fix while Val needed to hurry. She chose the wrong shoes for this walk and stumbled around like a drunk. In LA she always lamented the driving but once she hit the pavement painfully, she longed for her leather seats. The pace woke her up at least. Nothing gets blood pumping like a walk from Tribeca to Chinatown.

She arrived at a rusted door on a trash heaped street, which opened to stairs steeper than hers. On the third floor, a studio kept art projects in various stages of distress. A sculptor and a photographer shared the space with Ace. He'd painted his part white and hosted pet snails in one corner. His mattress was hidden behind a canvas. Every night he pulled it out and slept on the edge. He woke at dawn daily to avoid being caught. Ace was a squatter and the last living artist.

He never sold out or kissed ass, refusing any work that wasn't art related, he stayed starving. Down-and-out. Feeding birds before himself. He used to squat in Harlem but went to eviction court and lost. He'd been to jail sometimes. Recently on behalf of his Mexican ex. ICE cops were hassling him, so Ace spat at them and spent a night in the slammer. He said he did it out of principle. But after they divorced, Ace called immigration on him.

Ace was a Capricorn sun, Aries rising, Scorpio moon. Vengeful and disciplined. He wrote musicals, painted portraits and scared the shit out of everyone.

"Remember when I punched you?"

Ace grinned.

She went in for a hug. "Which time?"

He twisted the hug into a headlock.

She brought six donuts from Dunkin' and Ace ate three in a row. Powdered sugar, jelly and glazed.

"You're so thin I hate you," she said.

"I could be thinner." He lifted his shirt and sucked in his torso like crucified Jesus.

Ace would excel in LA, he was too handsome for New York. "Are you doing OK?" She regretted asking.

"Why wouldn't I be?"

"The divorce."

"Oh I've just thought of it as like, editing the 'personal life' part of my future Wikipedia page. I'm writing a musical about it."

She laughed. "Of course you are."

"It's called Gay Divorce." Ace got up and turned on his keyboard. It was painted white, including the black keys. Ace kept it by the window so he could see the street when he played. Ace always had an audience. The windowsill was blotted in bird shit. As he played for Val he spoke-sang like Patti Smith would.

"Let's all say GAY DIVORCE/ It's OK GAY DIVORCE/ He threw beer on my face/ He couldn't find peace/ Nostalgia pulled him away/ To the new shit/ A dark room with a dozen dicks/ Said he'd come back if I grow/ You'll come back for my smokes/ Don't cry on your way out/ Don't pout/ I'll miss your skid marks the most/ Let's all say GAY DIVORCE/ It's OK GAY DIVORCE/"

Val envied his talent but couldn't indulge in jealousy since she'd "made it." Ace didn't envy anybody. He knew there was enough to go around, it's just that what went around wasn't distributed fairly. Only a sucker could live in New York and say this town ain't big enough for the two of us.

She met Ace in college. Both poor, alternative and anorexic, they hooked each other at first sight. They created a shared psychosis and devoted themselves to it. Ace was too close and out of reach. Falling in love with someone dead would have been less painful. The friendship was incestuous and obsessive. Most nights she slept over until he made her move in. After his roommate left, citing harassment. Ace could be difficult, even hostile, but only the way a genius is. How could somebody so funny be anything less than a saint?

Through Ace she tasted the life she'd longed for. He was free. She couldn't predict a word he said or move he made. How his mind worked was a mystery. He made her feel conventional in comparison—but special. The chosen one. To Ace, all others were enemies. Those not surviving on rations or working with piety. Living in his world was exhilarating and full of purpose.

Counting coins for his coffee was more glamorous than anything red carpets led to. Ace made her his doll. He revolutionized her look and how she'd approach it from then on. She grew up shopping at thrift stores and mini malls. Her style was based on band posters and movie stars. She mixed her Balkan ideals and Appalachian reality. How should a woman look? Sexy. With a push-up bra, teased hair, tight pants, full face. The first thing Ace did was shave her head. "You're Tank Girl, not Debbie Harry." He tore up her clothes and styled them into avant-garde looks.

She became an intimidating *fag hag*—and had trouble getting laid. When she did find boys, Ace scared them away. He had as many boys as he wanted. Their shared lunacy had different rules for him. They ended up falling out. The root of the decay was unclear but festering for years.

As they grew, Val struggled to remain devoted. Ace was like her boyfriend, only they didn't have sex, and he wasn't in love with her, as she was with him. She had all the trappings of a romantic relationship and none of the perks. How long did he expect her to go on like this? To keep rejecting straight men for him? She pictured herself at fifty, waiting for Ace to leave a lover and come back to their home, decorated by him.

She tried forging a new kind of friendship, which allowed room for their separate lives. But their bond didn't work that way. The last thing he said to her was, "If I want to see you again, I'll know where to find you, on your knees in a bathroom."

Only a heart transplant would have eased her suffering. They didn't speak for years. She made the first move. After all, she owed her life to him.

"When do you leave?" Ace sat on the floor.

"Five days."

"Where you staying?"

"The Roxy."

"Must be nice."

She was used to feeling judged, but Ace missed the point. She was staying at the Roxy because that's the hotel Leonardo died in. And she wanted to sleep in the same room, lie in the same bed as him. If he really wanted to get into it, she could afford a nicer hotel.

"It's a work trip," she said flatly.

"I thought it was a funeral." He laid down and stretched.

"Memorial. We *were* working together."

"And?" He slid into downward-facing dog.

"And...I'm here for him."

"And...how will you work together if he's dead?" Plank.

"Well...the whole lit world will be at this thing."

"So you're networking at a memorial?" Corpse pose.

"It's not like that." Her voice skipped an octave.

Ace hopped up and walked to a corner. "I'm not judging." He shrugged, found a joint and lit it. "I only asked in case you're here for my play." He blew rings at her. "I wrote a part for you. Hooker rat."

"I'm flattered."

He paced the space. "You'll need to audition."

"You know I just met this rat in my hotel room."

"Is he your new boyfriend?"

"He's not my type."

"Too clean?"

"Too smart."

He snorted a laugh. She wished he'd linger in it but knew Ace directed moods and got bored of nice ones. "So you're riding a ghost for clout." The dynamic fell into place, with her at his mercy and him being merciful. When tension can't be resolved sexually, conflict resolution is infinite jest.

CHAPTER 9
JOKER IN THE PACK

She stepped out onto swarmed streets. Old ladies carried bags stuffed with cans on their backs like snail shells. Ace hadn't asked about her separation with Caleb. Straight divorce wasn't interesting.

Caleb didn't answer when she called. Soho shopping proved stressful. Sant Ambroeus was full and Opening Ceremony was closed. Canal Street fakes were uninspired.

Walks revived her, usually. You can walk away from anything, she always said. Anything but yourself. Walks trick you into believing you're moving forward, one way or another. That day, all she felt was bitter about being on her feet.

Walking in circles.

She returned to her room disillusioned. "I'm back," she called.

The Rat hopped out of the tub and stopped at her feet. His tail waved eagerly. She pulled a donut wrapped in tissue from her purse. In baby bites he devoured it. *My tiny tyrant*, she thought, fondly.

After he finished eating, he leapt onto the bed and she curled up next to him. Caleb didn't answer when she called, twice. With a big sigh she pulled out her tarot deck. Thinking of him, she closed her eyes and pulled a card in his name.

Seven of Swords. *Betrayal, deception and trickery.* "You got away with something?" she asked aloud.

The Rat turned and sneezed at her.

"Not you, dummy, my ex." He sniffed the cards curiously. "Want me to pull one for you?" *Shuffle, shuffle,* "You can ask the deck a particular question, or just do a general, card of the day, vibes of the moment sort of reading." *Shuffle, shuffle, shuffle.* "I usually do the latter."

She placed the cards in an accordion ring in front of him on the bed. "Now, pick one."

The Rat looked carefully at the options. After a few moments of consideration, the tip of his tail landed on a card. She pulled it out and turned it for them both to see.

"Ah!" she exclaimed. "The Fool, this one's my favorite! Lucky you. It means new beginnings and unlimited potential. It can be scary, of course. You need an open mind…I'm pretty sure you've got one. Just close your eyes and take a leap of faith, into the unknown." She laid the card by him and he chewed on a corner. "It can sound a bit trite, but some things are cliché because they're true." He jumped on her lap and patted his belly, as an instruction. "Not now," she said. "Actually, I need you to go to the bathroom. I must do something private."

He shook his head and sat in her lap.

"I know, you've seen me naked already. But this is not something you need to be around for."

He sighed, leapt off her and the bed and crawled under the chair across the carpet.

"That's fine, but no peeking."

She laid on her back and began masturbating with the crystal dildo from her bag.

She couldn't decide on a fantasy. The Australian walking his Siberian Husky on the beach? *Nah.* The barista at Blue Bottle? *Too young.* The surfer who carried his board shirtless? *Boring.* She was the Goldilocks of jerking off. The toy was bullshit; Venice Girl got it for her in Topanga, from the gift shop of the Inn of the Seventh Ray. "It used to be cool," Venice Girl would say. Val avoided Topanga, she hated hippies.

"The Inn was bought by reptilians a few years ago and it shows." Venice Girl slurped her Erewhon smoothie.

Val pulled on her grip socks. "How so?"

"The service is cold." Venice Girl stretched on her reformer, legs on the right, looking left, then legs on the left, looking right. "They're harmless but don't look them in the eye."

"What happens if you look them in the eye?" Val asked.

"I don't know, I don't do it!"

The stone BLOPPED *onto* the floor and she got on her belly.

She worked best when she got off with her hands, thinking of the man who raped her. In her head she called him Dior Homme. That's his scent. She still wasn't over him. What he did to her that day didn't wipe away the rest. Throughout her marriage he was her go-to highlight reel. She fought it at first, watched porn or tried thinking of others, futilely. She figured—with blue balls and a headache—why the fuck should I hold out on myself? If you can gain pleasure from pain, isn't that a victory?

It's not like she thought of *the incident* when she fantasized. It would interrupt another fantasy, sometimes, in flashes, like an intrusive thought, like when you're walking a dog over a bridge and think, what if I threw him. That happened rarely, enough to not deter her from indulging in *the times before* like an old VHS. Like a movie you cut off before the end, because the end sucks. She never finished *Ghost World* anymore or *Lost in Translation*. This was her *Titanic*, she only jerked off to the first tape of two.

She came with a grunt and fell asleep with her hands under her hips, slack-jawed.

When she woke up in the dark her arms were numb and her back sore. Drool stuck her face to the pillow.

Shivering on top of the covers, she opened her eyes to see The Rat nibbling the remaining half of The Fool card on the pillow next to her.

"Ugh, thanks for waking me."

She ordered room service, a vegan burger with extra vegan cheese, French fries and a Coke. The restricted-calorie diet she's been on since adolescence was void when traveling. Only a sicko wouldn't indulge in hotel fries. She delighted in the mini jars of ketchup and cloth napkins, which she chucked in her luggage. They sat together on the bed and took turns taking bites of carbs, fats and protein. By the time she was dressed, a handful of fries remained. "You can finish those, but you need to put the tray outside the door when you're done."

The Rat looked at her, then the tray, then her.

"I'm joking, you can make a mess, fight for your right to party!"

When the door shut behind her, The Rat held up an end of French fry in his hand, as if it were a cigar, and pretended to smoke.

CHAPTER 10
FLEUR DU NOIR

She hailed a cab in a cocktail dress, six-inch heels, a fake fur coat and a human hair wig. "Berlin." She was careful not to sit on the hairpiece, twisting it over one shoulder.

"This ain't an airplane."

"Avenue A and 2nd." She rolled her eyes.

Drivers these days just looked at maps, had no idea where anything was. Technology was to blame for all their problems, Val thought. Technology progresses while humanity stalls, withdraws, drools in a corner. She double-checked the location of the bar on Google Maps and saw its Tripadvisor reviews. Who wants to see photographs of what the inside of a bar looks like? Shouldn't that be a secret waiting to be discovered? Knowing about places used to be a social currency only night owls had. Word of mouth to mouth.

She scrolled the reviews and shook her head. "Psychopaths." Since when did people rate nightclubs? That makes as much sense as rating books. Anthony Bourdain can declare if a place is cool, and Quentin Crisp can suggest a novel. Their taste is based on exquisitely lived experience! But all these normies who know nothing and have nothing to do but slam culture as we know it—

The car halted and jolted her out of the spiral.

"Danke!"

As you could see from Google Maps, Berlin was a downtown bar with an underground music venue. But you could only know by going that something always went down there. The place had a style that inspired trouble. Iconic red curtains and black and white tiles made it *Twin Peaks* creepy. Dead-on for man-hunting and mind-losing. Electronic music seeped from corners and couples who had yet to dupe each other danced. Walking inside felt like casting a spell. She sat at the bar next to a man in a suit. Something told her this guy was holding.

"Got a bump?" She flipped her perfumed wig and let him get a whiff.

He bribed the bathroom attendant with twenties to let them share a stall. There he dropped to his knees and lifted her skirt. He put his head between her legs and kept it over her underwear. His breath burned as she scooped blow from a vial with a tiny spoon. People with coke hardware were such freaks.

"You from around here?" She looked down at his head.

"Boston," he exhaled.

She inhaled coke and watched his head bob between her legs. Submissive men were drawn to her despite her disgust for them. Maybe her hatred charmed them. The sight of this one repulsed her. Sex was just a power play. Men make love like greedy children, she thought. Straight women live in hell.

"You're pathetic," she told him.

He groaned in ecstasy, licking her Fleur du Mal underwear, an expensive pair, now ruined. Annoyed, she pulled them down and shoved them in his pocket. There she found a condom and handed it to him. Get this over with.

Her head rang with blow as she bent over the toilet. She felt more guilt about betraying her dealer than cheating on her husband.

. . .

Caleb didn't answer when she called in the cab home. He was screening her calls. Maybe he'd pick up if she rang from another line.

Trashed in the hotel room, she dialed her favorite phone number into the Roxy telephone.

The Man answered. "Yo. Who's is this?" She hung up, confused by her own mistake.

Lap, lap, lap. What's that sound? The Rat drinking out of the toilet. "Noooo, baby boy." She ran to the bathroom and lifted him from the bowl. "You want still or sparkling?"

She carried him to the fridge and let him peer inside. Undecided, she poured him a cup from each bottle. He drank a bit of both and turned to her, licking his lips. "Wanna watch TV before we pass out? When I'm this drunk it's hard to wind down."

They got under the covers, The Rat resting on her chest, his tiny heartbeat hitting hers like love's metronome. "Ooh, Jimmy Fallon. You know, I saw him perform once, ages ago, when he was opening for The Strokes. He was so cute back then. Jesus, I think I was like, fifteen. Anyway, now he's an alcoholic." The Rat nibbled her hair. "I know, I know, I'm one to judge."

Jimmy Fallon introduced the musical guest. "Please welcome the incredible Sock Sniffers!"

"No way, that's Caleb's old band!" The Rat looked up, alarmed. "They made it big right after he moved to LA. He always blamed me for that."

The guitarist started to riff and she threw the remote at him, cracking the screen.

CHAPTER 11
DREAM BOY'S NIGHTMARE

Daily Horoscope: Pisces:
A vision comes in the night.
Don't turn away, you are ready.
It's been waiting for you.

"Urgh." Sand Boy rolled desperately in his sleeping bag. Laying on his back strained his neck and turning onto his stomach hurt his knees. He stared at Val's empty house. Two nights he hadn't slept. Dreams never escaped him before. Turning the doze button on was his special power. He could close his eyes and shoot into space from wherever, whether it was a moving train or under a bridge, even face-down on the sidewalk. So what was wrong now? He scowled at her empty house.

Sand Boy got out of his bag and crept toward the dark. You're pointless, he told the water. Nice to look at, not to touch, unless you're a water person, as he called the local surfers. But even they wore wetsuits. Sand Boy hated the cold, that's what brought him here in the first place. He looked up and tried to find a constellation, but he couldn't tell one from the other. A song came to mind, something his dad would play in the car. Something about stars in the sky. Sand Boy hadn't talked to him in years. But it wasn't his fault, was it? How could he have taste in music and no sense of justice. How could he listen to Iggy Pop and be so closed-minded. Starry night. How could the man that took him on motorcycle rides be the same one that looked him in the face and said what he said. Iggy Pop was forever an underdog, always jealous of David Bowie. Imagine having it all and feeling that way. Sand Boy could imagine, he'd felt it, too. Being on top is the same as the bottom. Poverty frees you from social rules the same way excess wealth does.

Neither paid taxes, but only the rich were damned.

CHAPTER 12
BABY GUTTER

Daily Horoscope: Sagittarius:
Don't fear the feminine.
Nurturing is not weakness.

"I see you played while I partied." Val held up evidence and The Rat seemed to shrug. While she'd been out chain-smoking, he was chewing her jeans. These weren't any old Levi's, they were R13. The prized pants were leopard-print and limited edition. Val found the destruction while dressing for brunch. "I should be pissed but this kind of kills."

He watched her study her ass in the mirror. The holes were expertly scattered between her upper thighs and lower butt cheeks. "Were you a designer in another life? Or just gay?" She grabbed him by the belly and held up her palm, so they were eye-to-eye. His gaze was dark, deep and familiar. "Little genius." She kissed him between the ears. "I'm going to an excruciatingly excruciating brunch, wish me luck. I'd take you along, but it would bore you to death." She plopped him back on the bed and waved goodbye. "Ciao, baby boy."

Once she left, he jumped into her luggage and started digging. The goal was finding the softest, most luxurious spot. He could choose between fake fur, 100% cotton, Japanese denim or layers of silk underwear.

Nestled between stockings and panties, he daydreamed about a distant world and faded away, while she met Rachel the Virgo at Russ & Daughters Café. The white dining room resembled the inside of an icebox. Frigid air assured clients the fish wouldn't flip-flop on their plates. Perhaps the salmon was at bay, but the jacket you had to wear inside would end up reeking of onions.

"Simple pleasures shouldn't be fussy," Val chewed a *plain on plain*. "Like bagels, coffee or dick… Everything you need in life can be found in a bodega. Including the boy working there."

Rachel chopped through latkes. "Do you have bodegas in LA?"

"Gas stations are our bodegas." They weren't real friends anymore, they just kept up appearances out of respect for their past. How many people did this for each other? Psychological museum visits. She texted Rachel out of pity, after imagining her scrolling Instagram on some sad sofa and seeing a video of Val at a downtown dinner party.

Rachel would say to herself, "Val's in New York?" Her husband would ask from the kitchen, "What, honey?" And she'd yell, "Val is in the city, and she didn't tell me!" He'd come to the living room, frowning, "She'll hit you up, I'm sure." But in the back of his mind, he'd know his wife had lost her edge. Val didn't want to do that to them.

Little did she know Rachel had muted her months ago.

"I'd never live in LA. Why would anyone, unless they're in the industry?" Rachel asked, spitting coffee onto her chin, which crept down her collar. She tried wiping it off, which only made it puddle into a psych ward ink blot.

"I'm kind of in the industry. I had some directors sniffing my crotch once the film adaptation came out."

"Oh?" Rachel checked her phone under the table. "Who?" Acrylic nails went *tap, tap, tap.*

"Nobody you'd know. I wrote a script. But that went nowhere. I'm cursed!"

"How so?"

"People I work with be dropping like flies."

"Like Leonardo?'

"Not only. This guy, Al, was directing a film I wrote. *Heaven and Hell at The Standard Hotel.* We were working at The Standard Downtown, and I was living in Hollywood. Those are like, worlds apart. You wouldn't know. I didn't, either! So I showed up late a few times and he lost his shit. Totally went rabid. Like chill, why do you care so much about someone being ten minutes late? Are you listening?"

"Yeah, go on." Rachel looked up from her lap.

"About a month later he had an asthma attack. He lived in the hills, on one of those curvy roads. There's always construction, it's a mess. Anyway, he couldn't find his inhaler. He called the ambulance, but the construction trucks blocked the street, so they arrived like, six minutes late. He's been brain-dead ever since."

"Damn." *Tap, tap, tap.*

"Yeah, so, the point is, something in him *knew* that timing was life or death. That's why he got pissed at me! It wasn't personality, just premonition. It's fucking tragic, right? And it's idiotic to act like that *isn't* something we should pay attention to. The signs the universe sends us."

Rachel looked up from her phone and stared at Val's torso. She could sit across the table without a single roll of fat forming above or below her belly button. She wondered what her friend looked like naked. How she must admire her body in the mirror. She had no scars or mangled skin. An abyss spread between them. All they had in common was the time they were roommates.

Meeting for bagels was charity; did she have any idea what it took for Rachel to go out? To break away from the baby Val hadn't asked about? She hadn't heard a word her former roommate said and changed the subject with a compliment. "You look great, what do you do?"

"Cocaine." She hoped to provoke Rachel. She was a square, now, to be fair, she had always been square-curious.

"LOL." Rachel said *LOL* out loud instead of laughing. "Sobriety was the hardest part of pregnancy, then I popped her out and still can't drink because of my fucking breast milk. Billy won't let me feed her formula, you know, he reads too many articles."

"You aren't missing anything." *You're missing everything*, she thought.

"Getting pregnant was hard," she said bitterly. "It's fucked up, when you think about it. We're told all our lives to fear it, like it's the worst thing that can happen to us, because it will ruin our future. Then we arrive at our future, the future we were supposed to preserve ourselves for, and once we're there, everyone's like, why the fuck aren't you pregnant?"

"Hah, right."

"You should hurry, it does get tricky."

"Hurry with who?" She glared.

"Sorry, I forgot. I mean, I heard, I haven't read the book yet, you know, I've been busy creating life! Ha, ha. But I know about you and Caleb, that must be terrible. Anyway, he never seemed like father material. Maybe you and Ace could have a *Gayby*!"

"I never wanted kids, not since I was one."

"Yeah, well, you'll be old one day. And who will take care of you then?"

"As if kids surrounding your deathbed makes it comfier. You can't escape the end either way. I'd rather enjoy life till then."

"The party will stop, girl. Life isn't going to be fun

forever. You wanna be out clubbing at forty? Those *Friendsgivings* get sad."

"Regular Thanksgiving is sad. Relatives make each other miserable. It's been proven, women are happier when unmarried and childless. Only men benefit from it."

"Look, I'm not trying to talk you into anything. I care about you, and I don't want you to regret it when it's too late."

"I'd rather regret not having kids than regret having them."

"Nobody regrets having kids!" She laughed.

"Actually, there's this book, *Regretting Motherhood*, which handles the topic brilliantly. People use the concept of regret to scare women into breeding when lots of us regret getting knocked up but aren't allowed to say so! The concept is taboo and therefore kept secret, therefore there's this idea that women who regret becoming mothers don't exist. But they do." Val sipped her coffee.

"God, sorry I said anything. I'm just worried about you."

"Don't worry about me." She slammed the cup down. "Maybe I'll freeze my eggs."

"That's a great idea." Rachel sopped up the grease on her plate with a piece of bagel and tossed it into her mouth.

"I'm fucking with you. Anybody who thinks their genes are that important is demented. If you have that much money to spend, adopt one of the kids who need parents instead of going all *Brave New World* on yourself."

"That's not what that book's about. You don't have to use the eggs, if you don't want to. It's insurance. Paying for peace of mind that men are born with. Doing whatever you want without worrying that time is running out."

"Oh, I've explained to my biological clock what a book tour is."

Rachel was shredding her napkin into pieces and placing them in a pile. "You know, I'm finally getting back to my manuscript, the one I started in school."

"Which manuscript?" Val played with the cream cheese discarded from her bagel, smearing it on her plate.

"You know how I was always up typing in the wee hours, when you'd get home?"

"Oh yeah, why did you never go out with me back then?"

"Because I was working toward my degree in *literature*? Not all of us can drop out of school to party."

"You mean to work as a journalist, at a freakishly young age?"

"You weren't that young."

"Well, it feels like a lifetime ago. Congratulations on getting back into it though, I hope your book brings you all the glory mine did." Val's book had only brought pain, she thought everyone knew that, but the look on Rachel's face said otherwise. "Hey, I'm kidding. It got no glory. Only glory holes."

Rachel perked up. "Speaking of glory holes, I can see your pussy through those jeans."

"Oh, that's The Rat." She slurped the last of her coffee, which was cold.

"The Rat? Is that some designer?"

"No, he's a literal street rat I'm living with. Now that you mention it, I asked him just this morning if he was a designer in a past life." It didn't matter if Rachel thought she was unhinged. Val realized in that moment she'd never see her again. Surprisingly, the idea filled her with dread.

"Are you OK?" Rachel waved in her face.

"No." She snapped out of it. "But writers shouldn't be."

"Right." Rachel raised her hand for the check. "I have to get back." The bill arrived and Rachel made a big show of paying. "I got this. I know those royalty checks only go so far." She slid a black credit card between them, with her husband's name written on it. The girls met eyes and felt bad for each other. "How's the new book going?" Rachel offered.

"It needs a new home, without Leonardo. I'm desperate for an agent, or another publisher crazy enough to sign me without one. I should be sending out my manuscript, but I can't stand to see it. I should trash it and write something new, but I'm stuck."

While Val talked, the waitress scanned Rachel's husband's card. "Uh-huh?"

"So I do this exercise. I take a sentence in one language, and I try to use the same letters to make a sentence that makes sense in another language."

"Wow." She signed and left a tip.

"Nikad se neću vratit u moj rodni grad. It means, I'll never return to my birth town."

"Okay..." Rachel started getting her things together like a schoolkid who heard the bell while the teacher was still teaching.

"Tough. Croatian. Eventually I got: Kin said cunt tit rave nod or drag."

"What does it mean?" She stood up.

"Nothing."

"Does it help you write?"

"Not really."

CHAPTER 13
TIME MACHINE

Daily Horoscope: Aries:
If you let it happen, you'll be happy.
But is that what you seek?
Don't listen to anyone but the rain.

The Man spent more time in his car than an Uber driver. After a decade of deliveries, he knew the streets like his kids. He had love for exits and bridges. Took longer routes to enjoy the curves. Los Angeles was a pinball machine, and his car was the ball. The machine tosses the ball up, down and all around until it falls into the hole. You need coin to start over.

After dreaming of wet cement, he woke one day with heavy legs. Lifting them off the bed was painful, walking to the bathroom was agony, his muscles were stiff and they burned with effort. He sat on the can and probed his knees, which were swollen and warm, pumped with hot fluid. When he pressed one side of his kneecap the other expanded. "Walking it off" only made it worse. An unbearable week passed before he caved to Zocdoc. By then his knees barely fit in his jeans. A doctor diagnosed him with reactive arthritis, but his treatments didn't work. Roids and painkillers only eased the symptoms, and he didn't want a habit. He knew fiends too well. Val suggested acupuncture, one of those nights she was extra chatty and bugged him at a red light. Don't tell a cokehead your problems unless you want their advice. The bitch came through though, she swore this dude fixed her back. "It's sketchy but worth it. No insurance no problem."

Her plug was in Korea Town. The Man rang the buzzer, and a Chinese man answered. Dr. Wu didn't bother dressing like a doctor, he looked like an undercover cop trying to pass for an accountant. Wordless, he led The Man up three creaky flights of stairs. His studio was a sweltering attic with a desk, two chairs and an examination table. The Man told Dr. Wu what his Zocdoc told him. Dr. Wu shook his head like, *Western bullshit*. "Take your pants off and lay on your stomach."

The Man winced as needles pierced his legs. Dr. Wu sprinkled spikes across his thighs and calf muscles. He added a cluster behind each knee. "You've got Taxi knees." He said. "Drivers have this problem, and women who wear heels every day." The needles in his legs were attached to wires, which led to a car battery. Val didn't tell him this part. "You ready?" Dr. Wu asked only hypothetically and turned on the box. The Man shook all over. As the shocks went off, he could smell his legs frying but it was just the restaurant downstairs.

Half an hour later he left the table slick with sweat. It took six sessions to feel normal. Dr. Wu said he wouldn't need to come back if he practiced his stretches. Dr. Wu taught him on the street, with a menthol squashed by his lips, "Step on a curb with one leg, heel hanging off, then press your heel down to the pavement, only your toes touch the curb, lean forward and hold the pose, count to fifteen, you should feel it from the back of your knee to your ankle, that sting, it's a good thing, alternate legs, and repeat ten times."

The Man never skipped a day.

He parked on a client's block and texted, "Ready." This client was always late. The Man pictured him jerking off since the kid was always in a bathrobe. He got out of the car and did his curb stretches. As he counted, he fingered Val's wedding ring in his pocket. He found it the other day; it must have slipped off during the hand-off. It wasn't unlike her, she was messy and jittery. It made him uneasy. He hated when she over-shared and made passes at him. Still, he owed her for the Wu tip. He didn't forget favors. He'd go back to her place and return it. "Yo, I found your gold in my car. I'll swing by to drop it."

CHAPTER 14
BLOOD KITCHEN

> Daily Horoscope: Sagittarius:
> Follow the reason, not the outcome.
> Don't turn your back on yourself.
> Violet clouds.

Val woke up feeling gnarly because she'd gone to Joe Allen in Hell's Kitchen after seeing Rachel. Down there she always felt pretty, around no-nonsense men with important jobs who drank pints between meetings.

After a couple drinks a bald one sat next to her at the bar. He smelled like Dior Homme, a cologne that didn't belong to him. Dior Homme was nothing like Dior Sauvage, a scent reserved for scumbags. Her Man, the one she was still obsessed with, he wore Dior Homme. The formula was crafted for rebels, (pretty) bad boys, motorcyclists in Burberry trenches. Either this man was clueless about how wrong he was for the perfume—maybe his wife had got it for him, hoping for a miracle—or he had the audacity to think he pulled it off.

She scoffed and shook her head, lost in silent insults.

He turned and said, "You turn me on." It was audacity, then. She put her hand on his leg, and said "Go to the toilet, imagine me pissing on you and don't come back till you cum." She didn't think he had it in him, but he stood silently and disappeared into the men's room. Five minutes later he returned, flustered, claiming that was the first time he ever did something like that. Red-faced, head down, he paid both their tabs and scrammed.

When she couldn't stand right anymore, she laid down in the back of a taxi. The driver hit on her and she let him, the usual questions, where are you going looking like that, all alone, where's your boyfriend, how is that possible, you've got such nice legs, they drive me crazy.

She smiled, said my hotel room, no boyfriend, awe thanks, and then he reached back while looking at the road, and grazed her thighs with his fingers. He only asked if he could after the fact.

She said you'll kill us if you drive like that. He swerved into an alley and parked, climbed into the back seat and pulled his dick out. It was already fat and throbbing.

With the meter running, she stayed horizontal and let him put her legs in his lap. He rubbed his dick on her thigh until he came somewhere, she wasn't sure. It turned her on which was so rare these days, and she was sorry to be too drunk to get off, and she reminded herself to remember the encounter the next the next time she jerked off, but already knew her brain would black-out the memory.

I guess this is what they mean by living in the moment.

She gave him a big tip and wondered if that's how men feel when they pay for sex.

When she walked into the hotel room, The Rat didn't judge her for crawling into bed on her hands and knees. She begged him for peanuts or potato chips, so he brought her both.

They shared the snacks and spread crumbs everywhere.

She got under the covers, still clothed, and before he got in himself, he scurried around her shoulders and legs, creasing the blanket, tucking her in. "Are you really real?" She slurred, eyes rolling back in her head. "If you are, you're my best friend." He confirmed his existence by biting her nose.

To fall asleep, she didn't count sheep; she counted the men she'd slept with. They led her to another nightmare. The tsunami chased her on Highway 101. It followed her from behind and all sides. Wherever she turned there it was, wet hell reaching heaven. For once, there were no cars on the freeway, just her and the wave.

She woke up soaked. The Rat watched her peel off sweaty clothes with a groan.

With one hand she called room service and the other reached for his belly, but he jerked away from her touch.

"What's up with you?" He curled into a fist. "I can't believe I have to leave the room today," she told him. "I feel awful. But Pie is too special to flake on. You'd love him. He's a rapper. Not my kind of music, I'm a rock 'n' roll girl. What are you into?" The Rat sighed. "Ok, I won't bother you until you've eaten." He watched her walk to the bathroom, then closed his eyes and heard the shower running. Then, Val's voice singing "My Way," the Sid Vicious version. Under the water she tried blocking images of the previous night. She sang so loud she barely heard the banging door.

"How long have you been waiting?" The bellboy wasn't moved when she opened the door, holding a hand towel over her body. Water droplets smeared her signature on the check. The Rat didn't look up as she set the tray down. "Your Majesty?" Her finger poked his ribs, so he opened his eyes, sniffed at the food, and tucked his nose into his belly.

"What's wrong?" She asked. The usual twinkle was gone from his eye. He had a dull, worn-out look, like he hadn't slept. "Rough night? I know mine was!" Sitting next to him, she ate ravenously, soaking through the small towel. Top-tier hangovers mixed with shame unlock the stomach's abyss. Val told The Rat what she'd gotten up to, hoping to entertain. When he yawned, she snuck scrambled egg into his mouth. He spat it out, hissed at her, leapt off the bed and disappeared behind the fridge. She felt sorrow.

"You think I'm gross now, is that it?" Her mouth spilled food. He didn't run back to her, to comfort her, to tell her, *no, I could never think that. How could you think I could think that about you? When you're so wonderful, and I'm just a rat.*

His tail didn't wave bye when she left this time.

In the elevator, she figured he was depressed but couldn't say why. Wasn't he living a rodent's fantasy? Sharing a fancy hotel room with a girl who paid for his food? But what did she know, and who was she to judge, as she was living a human's fantasy, and wanting to end that, too.

Through the lobby she passed hookers waiting for Johns, businessmen trying to scam someone, waiters waiting for a break.

She pushed through the front doors, against the wind. The world telling her to stay in. New York City showed no mercy. The air slapped her like a sour lover. Nobody smiled back at her. She was grateful that day to live in LA. People were cruel there, as they are anywhere, but their blows felt softer in sunlight. You can isolate yourself in LA and avoid the gross reality of humanity. The only catch in that case is being stuck with your own.

For Val self-pity is a warm pool always welcoming you to dip your toes in and she was torso-deep. She longed to plunge, total immersion, a day spent wallowing, but before she could do that, she had a date with another gay man.

"Hey, city slicker." Pie turned at her tap on his shoulder and crushed her in a hug. He was a six-foot queer Scorpio rapper from Queens she'd interviewed during her *GooGoo* days. Their catty Q&A led to friendship—one of the last, elusive perks of journalism. He was avant-garde inside and out, and liked Val despite himself.

He looked her up and down and said, "I thought you lived by the beach?"

"I do."

"Your ass is paler than ever."

"I sleep during the day." She shrugged.

"Twirl for me." He instructed with a finger, and she spun like a music box ballerina. "Nice jeans, I can see your whole cunt through them."

"Thanks, the holes cost extra…not that hole, though, that one's free!"

"How are you so annoying?"

"I have no choice, it's my factory settings."

Pie twirled next, Rick Owens black silk sucking up sun. He always stunned, his line being, *you don't have to get ready if you stay ready.* "I can't believe you dragged my tired old ass out here." He shook his head. Pie couldn't refuse free lunch at the Odeon. Val would only cross boroughs for Caleb and knew she had to bribe Pie to do the same.

Pie avoided Manhattan since it became a haven for the old and wealthy, rather than the young and broke. He hung around spots like a mood ring, for the horny and woke.

The Odeon was nice enough to feel fancy but not upscale enough to be ugly. They slid themselves into a booth by the bar. In the booth next to theirs, a group of skaters discussed surgery. Pie and Val listened while scanning the menus. "I got this cartilage from a dead man in my knee and it's changing my personality…" Val had the urge to write down what the skater was saying and turn it into a story. "I have new cravings, new fears…" Maybe she'd write it this week, and send it to *The New Yorker*…

"I'm Mike, I'll be taking care of you." Inspiration interrupted.

"I'll have the steak, medium rare, fries, and a vodka martini."

"And I'll do the creamed spinach and mashed potatoes…and a dirty vodka martini, extra olives."

The waiter took their menus.

"Now I feel bad splurging, you only got sides."

"I'm not that hungry, I ate room service with my Rat."

"Your what?"

"There's a Rat in my hotel room. We're close, or we were, he hates me today."

"You know what? No." He looked around. "These drinks better come fast and hit hard." He clapped his hands, startling the skaters.

"Like my exes." Val laughed.

"Speaking of exes, what happened?" He lifted a brow.

"Jesus, no foreplay?"

"Want me to spit in my hand and rub it on you? Damn." Being separated by flyover states for years couldn't kill their momentum. "Come on, spill."

"Well, we had lots of problems." She perked up at the waiter approaching their booth. "But I think that deep down, he hated women."

"Val, I hate to break it to you." Pie took the drinks from the server and handed one to her. "Everyone does. Cheers."

Clink. "This wasn't the standard Good Boy Misogyny." *Sip*. "He thought everything I did was insane, hysterical, *female*. The more he got to know me, the less human I was. It's usually the other way around, right? He only understood the version of me he'd created in his head.

When you're just starting to know someone and can still project fantasies onto them? I could feel him start to reject me. Not just my body but my soul. And his recoiling unleashed my self-loathing."

"This is so good." Pie said into his vodka. "Go on."

"My whole 'thing' is my personality. I *am* a personality, right? Well, he thought my personality was witchcraft." She swallowed an olive and coughed.

"If you choke, I'm not getting the check."

"Sorry—" *Gulp, Gulp, Gulp.* "That's better." *Burp.* "When I eat, it's like, fuck around and find out."

"So…he thought you were a witch."

"I was…a foreign object. And instead of being into that, the way I'm in awe of how he plays music—it turns me on because I *can't* do it myself—he took what he 'didn't get' as a threat. From my writing to my small talk."

"Wait." Pie drained his drink, handed the empty glass to a server and asked for another. "Continue."

"One night, we were at this obnoxious dinner, and I was winning over the host, who's a total sociopath, and Caleb was like, I can't believe you like that guy! I was like, Caleb, are you kidding? That's just me being a fake ass bitch! Which I need to know how to be. To survive."

"I know that's right."

"He's like, you fooled me, I thought you really liked him. He seemed hurt. I was like, honey, once you learn to fake an orgasm during rape, complimenting ugly shoes is a piece of cake. And he goes, how do I know you're really laughing at *my* jokes? All paranoid and shit."

Pie cackled. "These boys are tragic."

"Beyond. It's a dumb example. I can't think of other examples because it happened constantly. He'd make me feel crazy or guilty over my…fucking…personality. Which I'm proud of by the way? It's easy for him to say. Easy for him to be like, why can't you just be honest about who you are, and what you think, blah, blah, blah."

"He doesn't know what a hoe has to do to get home at night."

"Right! And aside from that, he thought it was wrong that I'd ever hang out with other guys in any capacity. Even professionally. He'd say, I'd never hang out with a girl without you. And I'd ask, is that because you don't think girls are worth hanging out with unless you're fucking them? Or because you can't trust yourself to hang out with a girl without fucking her? Either way, it's your problem!"

Pie got his new drink and sipped patiently. "Mm."

"Guys who say men and women can't hang out without having sex are the reason sexism persists, like, it's easy for men to say they won't hang out with us, out of the bedroom, because that doesn't ruin their lives, that doesn't cut them off from society! But if I could only hang out with girls or gays, how could I ever get ahead? Like no offense to you or me, but it's a straight man's world. And if we aren't allowed to hang with them, we're stuck behind." Val realized she was yelling. The skater table stopped talking. One of them cleared his throat.

"I never hang out with straight men. I don't think I know any. I don't know what they do…where are they? I can't see them." Pie rolled his eyes at the skaters, and they went back to chatting.

"Well, the gays have their own self-contained, sustained, maintained universe. But I can only be an emotional support fag hag in it."

"Sorry, honey. I do know what you mean. But it's a shame. I was sad to hear the news. I liked you two together. He was so cute. And charming."

"Yeah. It wasn't always bad, otherwise I wouldn't have married him. But once that resentment shows its face, even Pat McGrath can't conceal it."

"I never saw him disrespect you, not even interrupt you, at least not around me."

Why didn't Pie understand he wasn't allowed to say

anything nice about Caleb? Those were the rules of engagement at this lunch. Why was she paying for his steak? Girls would know better. "Sorry I'm talking so much. What's going on with you?" Her chest ached as she drank more to keep her voice from shaking. As a waiter passed, she tapped their arm for a refill.

"Girl, don't ask, I work at a supermarket."

"What do you mean?"

"I mean I'm a cashier at a supermarket."

Val didn't know what to say. If she showed shock, it would imply Pie's situation was bad, but if she didn't, it would imply it was good. Which it wasn't. There's nothing wrong with working at a supermarket, but there was so much wrong with Pie doing so. One of the great rappers of their generation swiping bar codes? She sipped her cocktail and cautiously asked, cool as possible, "How did that come about?"

"Bitch you can say it. What the fuck, right?"

"Dude, what the fuck."

"I broke my ankle. Had to skip the Euro tour… I was meant to close Berghain! Now I close bodegas. What can I say? It's a fickle industry. Kids forget you quick."

"But you're the blueprint. None of these clowns would exist without you."

"They've got no respect for their elders." Pie winked at her.

Their food arrived. "You calling me old?"

He eyed her sides. "Food so soft you can take your dentures out."

"Ha-ha." She poured Ketchup onto her mashed potatoes and stirred them into a pink paste. "So, what now?"

He dipped a few fries into her dish, said, "There's something very grotesque about this," and ate them. Between bites he spoke. "Usually, I'm like, what's the point. These gay artists today, their focus is how gay they are, online, at least. The performance of it all. Being a queer artist rather than an artist who happens to be queer. 'Identity' is their thing, but it's not their own. They never had to create an identity *offline*. They never had to survive on the street. Never sucked dick in an alley! They've got rich parents; they accept being paid in 'exposure.' They're ruining it for the rest of us. I don't see why I should fight them."

"Don't let the bastards win." She stole a few of his fries. He was focused on the meat.

"Not an option. Look, I tell myself I'll quit music every day, and yet I find myself with a new EP! Hah! And it's fire, Val. My best work yet. Puts the Zoomers to shame. I just need Botox before I shoot my next video. Speaking of…who did yours?"

"What are you talking about? Keep drinking, blurred vision hides wrinkles." Her phone buzzed in her lap. She looked down at it and yelped. The skaters had enough of them. One wearing a beanie asked for the check.

"If you just got good career news you can keep that to yourself." Pie said.

"No, my career died with Leonardo."

"So, who's texting you? New boo?"

She wrote The Man back describing where he could find a spare key. What a bummer, she timed this badly. Real bimbo behavior, but better than nothing. This would be romantic. *Feel free to hang out, make yourself at home*, she texted, shaking at the thought of him opening her underwear drawer. "It's my drug dealer, actually."

"Girl, it's barely noon."

"I'm not copping. He's in LA, he found my wedding ring in his car and he's going to leave it at my place."

"Damn that's one honest dealer. He could have pawned it."

"No need to, he's loaded."

"I got into the wrong business."

"You and me both."

CHAPTER 15
GUTS AND GLASS

Daily Horoscope: Pisces:
They don't tell you
because they're afraid what you'd do.
It's never too late to give up.

Sand Boy's head rang with Val's voice as he stared at her windows. *I'm going out of town, would you like to house-sit?* What a bitch. He resented her for this dilemma.

Since she left, he hadn't slept and those three white nights were puzzling. He was used to her light and now he was screwed. Sleep was his safety, another world he could pop into when he was tired, bored or hungry. He was so bored. He stared at her windows.

A girl skateboarded past him then stopped abruptly. She stood and thought for a second, then skated back to him and slammed the tail. The deck scraped the pavement meeting the sand. She took off her hoodie while balancing.

"Here." She held the hoodie out.

"Nah." Sand Boy turned in his bag to face away from her. He didn't want to see the letdown on her face. Why'd people get their feelings hurt so easily? After a pause her wheels skidded across concrete, close then far away. Did he look like he needed a hoodie, of all things? Nobody held cash anymore. The Godless city was going cashless. Paper money was dirty and inching toward illegal. Having it was a sign that your work was illegal, that you were illegal. They say cashless is "eco-friendly," but are people not eco? What about people like him? What about immigrants and hookers? He'd rather die than make a sign advertising his Venmo. Signs were lame. Sand Boy never had to beg, he'd just sit somewhere and people would bring him things. He was good-looking under his dirt, but that wasn't it. His passiveness won people over. The *not*-begging, the letting people think it was their idea to help him. No matter where you end up, they're the same. Some people gave for credit. If he didn't make eye contact, didn't nod thanks, they'd take it back. Others asked questions. What will you do with this? Why should I help you?

Prove it. Some offered cruelty under the guise of advice. Needy givers hurt more than avoiders. Those who walked by with averted eyes. People minding their own business didn't offend him. It's not like they owed him anything. Those who crossed the street and held their breath tried to make a point to themselves. *That could never be me.* But they knew it could. They were all barely scraping by. Violence was expected but mainly he was left alone. Mostly he was embarrassed for everybody.

Sand Boy got up and followed the skater. Venice was once a refuge for hustlers, drifters and cannibals. These days it was a playground for yuppies in Lululemons. The skate park was the last safe space for his kind. Mike, the old veteran in the wheelchair, was never not there. Parked by the railing with the ocean view he watched the skaters from dawn to dusk. He stayed shirtless to show off battle scars on his chest. Deep wrinkles were framed by a yellow beard. He heckled the kids and they called him Chief. "You got more work to do!" He'd yell when someone smacked themselves, and when he wasn't yelling, he was laughing.

Sand Boy borrowed a chick's board and skated barefoot. Old-school, Dogtown style. He wasn't so different from the other bowl boys but he knew she knew he was homeless. The others wore clean Dickies and smiled white. Skaters get lots of credit for being athletes but skating's just fearlessness. There's no way around pain and eating concrete's no joke. So many kids quit after their first fall. So that's tip number one, be tough, accept the hurt. Two, don't jump ship. When you're bombing a hill and start to wobble, get that tickling feeling on your feet, the sick feeling in your gut, don't fight it. Instinct says get off what's wobbling. Instinct is what stands between boys and legends. Keep your feet on the board no matter what and you're good. Skating is simple. Some do it, others live it. Most can't. Once you manage, it's bliss. When everyone's cheering, even when you don't land your trick, even if you twist your ankle, the hype is worth living for.

On the boardwalk he passed the camps and waved to his comrades. Tents were comfortable and neighbors could be helpful. Shelter was tempting but he knew better. He once had a whole tent for himself under the I-405, off Venice. A row of tents on each side of the bridge. Community can be a trap. Even the unhoused get picky, form cliques, act no better than the assholes in ties. He was better off alone, under the girl's window. He hit the water fountain and toilets. The pavement burned more than usual so he went toward the waves. He walked in the wet sand and when he reached his sleeping bag, he was exhausted, but still not sleepy. Her dark windows taunted him to come in.

CHAPTER 16
MURDER SUICIDE

Fueled by two martinis and a text from her Man, she took the train with Pie. "Is this a good idea?" He asked, balancing without touching the poles, which he found gross. Val tried doing the same and stepped on feet.

"Oops, sorry! What?"

"Can you handle this?"

"Seeing him? Who knows. Either I can handle it, and I survive, or I can't, and I die. Each outcome is fine." She had to see Caleb, to *amicably* sign the papers together… they weren't technically divorced yet. That was her official reason. The real reason was that something soft inside her hoped seeing him would answer a question. The one that tortured her soul. *What have I done?* "This is as good a time as any. At least I'm already buzzed!" On the corner of Greenpoint and Kent they kissed goodbye.

"Call me if you need anything. But I'll be at work. So, I won't answer."

Pie went off one way and she walked the other, down gusty streets, haunted by memories, toward his apartment.

Knock, knock. "It's me…your favorite cautionary tale."

Caleb was back at his old place, where they'd fallen in love. She could let herself in uninvited, as he never locked the doors. Often, he'd left the key hanging from the doorknob as a dare. It was something they used to fight about.

"Go away!" He warned from the living room.

She walked past enemy lines into the memory trap. The smell of his clothes knocked the wind out of her. A shadow of their love still lived there, shriveled and starving. If she got close it could maim her.

"You can't just show up unannounced."

"I didn't want to, but you don't answer my calls." She crept through the hallway past the tiled kitchen. She'd loved how the floors were warped, like they were built on a wave. His sink was a disaster of dishes. He used to joke about his filth. "You have it all, my empire of dirt." The time she wasted cleaning up after him wasn't funny.

She made it to the living room, where he sat on the sofa cross-legged. His face left her speechless. Caleb had always been too healthy for her. He had a good appetite, worked out, and slept regularly. He was fresh-faced and wholesome. Their separation had turned his skin green. His eye bags were violet, and his face was chiseled. The excess fat was drained. He was all jawline and fisheyes. Like a YSL model. Caleb shifted on the couch and crossed his arms to shield his heart. A slow explosion went off in her gut. She held the wall behind her for support—one step farther and she'd be a puddle of blood.

"You're drunk," he declared.

"I wouldn't come sober."

"What do you want?"

"I want to talk."

"I've read everything you have to say."

"Okay, that's fair." She shifted her weight. "What do *you* have to say?"

"As if you care."

"I care about you, come on."

He laughed. "You put me through actual hell."

She hated when people used "actual" as an intensifier. Like *what the actual fuck*. It made the phrase lose effect.

"You know who you married."

"Apparently not."

"What did you expect, then. What did you want from me?"

"I just wanted you, Val." Her name in his voice was lethal.

"Bullshit."

"The Val I met. Not whoever this is."

"You wanted fun me." She sighed. "When things were easy, we had fun. When things weren't easy, we stopped having fun. We weren't enough for each other without the fun."

"It was never easy with you."

"Hah. My parents are immigrants. You don't under—"

"Here we go."

"—stand real struggle. They stuck together through that. But I hurt your feelings? You know how many women stand by their nasty husbands? You couldn't stick around because of my book? I'm an artist, I must tell the truth. It hurts sometimes."

"You're not an artist, you're just a bitch."

"Why can't a girl be both?" She didn't understand why they were being so cruel. Why couldn't they be tender and genuine? They shared so much, their own little world still existed somewhere, they could jump back into it. Only through violence could they survive. They'd fall apart if one gave into softness.

"How can you joke about this?" His eyes turned red. "Our marriage isn't a political statement. My life isn't your feminist manifesto."

"My readers would disagree." *Gross show of pettiness, Val. Is this who you want to be?*

"You can't just be an asshole and rack it up to *women's rights*."

"Says who?"

Caleb made a fist by his mouth and pretended to bite it. The ugly gesture amplified her disgust. He'd punch walls, slam doors and raise his voice. He'd grab her arms, so his fingers left marks, push her into a wall or raise his arm above her head as if to strike. Resisting took effort and he wanted her to appreciate that he didn't smack her across the mouth. She didn't care. If he hit her, she'd have a reason to hate him. "Right and wrong is like science." He mused. "The truth doesn't need you to believe in it for it to exist."

"Women don't have the luxury of right and wrong."

"The fuck does that mean?"

"When a man cheats it's wrong because it's cliché. It happens all the time since the beginning of time, and nobody questions it. Abuse of power within an abusive power structure *he* created."

"Oh, shut up."

"When a woman cheats it can be wrong, but it can also be rebellion, centuries in the making. It can be for all the women who suffered before her!"

"Infidelity turns everyone into a philosopher."

"Our grandmothers all watched their men sleep around while they cleaned their house-jail and raised brats they never wanted. Sometimes a woman's infidelity can be right..." She paused and chose her next words carefully. "Especially if she begged her husband to fuck her."

"Sorry I didn't degrade you!" Veins bulged in his neck. "All you so-called feminists want is to be treated like whores."

He had no idea what he was talking about.

I hate you. I hate you. I hate you.

He glared at her and she avoided his eyes and turned hers to his bookshelf. He didn't own a copy of *Malibu Babylon*. But holy shit, there it was. This upset her more than anything he'd said. She stomped toward the shelf and pulled it out. "You bastard." She clutched *Hollywood Babylon* to her chest.

"You cunt." He wept into his hands. "I would have died for you."

She sighed and plopped on the couch. It's easy to tell someone what you would have done, you'd make the ultimate sacrifice but not do the dishes or give a compliment not dripping in insult. She sat far enough to not smell him—his scent would cloud her focus—and close enough to touch his shoulders. They were bouncing as he cried.

"The kindest thing we can do for each other is move forward. Like…two people in line at the bodega."

Caleb rubbed his eyes. Her hand dropped from his shoulder to his knee. He put his hand over hers. Outstanding hands calloused from drumming.

"Remember before you ever wrote that damn book we used to fantasize about it. We'd get high and read one-star Amazon book reviews out loud to each other, laughing so hard we pissed ourselves. You said even if it flopped, you'd be happy that you wrote it."

"Of course I remember." The early days with Caleb were responsible for her laugh lines.

"I hope you're happy."

"I'm not." She said sharply.

"Don't say that." He grabbed her hand off his knee and threw it at her face as if it weren't attached to her body.

She flinched at the gesture. "I thought you'd like to hear that."

"If *you* aren't even happy then all this suffering was pointless."

"Suffering is never pointless."

He sighed. "Alright, let's get this over with."

"The papers are in my purse." She sniffed.

"By the way, I can see your pussy through those jeans."

CHAPTER 17
GOOD TIME GIRL

Sand Boy shoved his sleeping bag into his backpack and slung it over one shoulder. He walked fifty feet to her house. Val wasn't the only voyeur of the two. She'd stare at him when she couldn't sleep, wound up by drugs, or nerves, and by the time she'd wind down the sun would come up and Sand Boy would open his eyes. He'd keep them on her as she slept through the day. Her gaping windows a silver screen into her life. Not much to witness, but the devil's in the details, one of the details being where she kept an extra key. He thought well she did invite me. If she was high when she did that's not my problem. High people are honest. In vino veritas, in coca candor. To the right of the welcome mat which said "cum inside" was a potted cactus. He lifted the vase to find a bronze key. Close up he saw white muck lining the cracks, it was blow, no doubt. He chuckled. They did the same drug. Hers more expensive and less effective. He looked over his shoulder for narcs. Just an old lady with a dog. When they passed he crammed the key inside the keyhole.

"This place rips." He surveyed the scene. Val's house was feminine and clean. Stylish furniture and art meant to impress guests that never came. Sand Boy was the first person to visit aside from her maid. He left his backpack on her sofa and made his way to the kitchen, scattering sand with each step. He was starving. The stainless-steel fridge was lined with Evian, Chardonnay, prosecco and IPA. He grumbled. Of course Val only ate out. Gelato and Grey Goose lived in the freezer. He took the ice cream and vodka upstairs.

Entering the bedroom he'd watched so often was uncanny. Like meeting an actor in real life and learning they're mini. Candle smoke and incense tainted the walls with a lingering odor. Outfits that didn't make the cut had been thrown around while packing. Her desk held stacks of *New Yorkers*, her new manuscript and sticky notes plotting an unfinished pilot. A hardcover copy of *Malibu Babylon* served as a paperweight. The movie poster hung above. He gazed at her bed, unmade and inviting. He'd get clean before jumping in, he owed her that much.

Sand Boy put the ice cream and booze on a stack of fashion magazines that served as a bedside table and walked from hardwood to marble. Her bathroom was the nicest part of the house. To him it was a castle. A bug on the tub startled him. Sand Boy hated bugs. You would too if you had to share your bed with them. You would too if you found them in your food. He looked for a weapon. A magazine lay by the toilet and he rolled it up. The Bug Assassin made his move.

WHAM!

The Bug Assassin inspected his seize. You gotta make sure they're dead. The only thing worse than a live bug is a bug that survived your attack and wants revenge.

"What the hell?" The bug wasn't a bug. The bug

was fake eyelashes. They stuck to the magazine, which he tossed in the trash.

The tub was enticing but Sand Boy knew he'd turn it into a mud bath. He turned the shower on scalding. It took him a few minutes to get it right. Val had one of those enormous square shower heads stuck to the ceiling which worked like rain. He stepped under the downpour and stood still. Venice Beach had free showers but those were violently cold and short. You had to keep pressing the button every few seconds, just to feel like you're being hosed off by the cops. Val's shower was blissful. And nobody was waiting in line to use it after him.

When his head cleared, he soaped his limbs into a lather. Scrubbed between toes and butt cheeks. The water funneled brown beneath him, then gray and clear. He washed and conditioned his tangled hair. Val's products were lush and her towels were fluffy.

Twenty minutes later he felt pampered. In the mirror, a glistening movie star stared back. Sand Boy dug under the sink. He found a fresh toothbrush and used it to clean his teeth. When he ran his tongue over his gums it reminded him of getting his braces off. The inside of his mouth was slimy and foreign. His skin felt tight. He slathered a fistful of La Mer over his face. It felt sick so he grabbed another two fistfuls to moisturize his body. His skin soaked up two hundred dollars of luxury cream like a thirsty plant. His harsh tan turned supple. He blow-dried and brushed his hair—a painful ordeal—and found himself with a golden mane. Flowing locks fit for the cover of *The Sports Illustrated Swimsuit Issue*. He stared at his clothes on the floor. A pile of dirt. He couldn't put those on now. Her walk-in closet called. The walls were lined with lightning bolts. Rows of shoes, handbags, dresses and jackets were organized by color.

"What a psycho," he mumbled, fondling the fabrics.

He pulled out a powder blue Miu Miu slip and threw it over his head. It fit nicely and created a smooth silhouette, accenting the bulge between his legs. He opened her underwear drawer and pulled out a pair of white satin panties. Those were snug but the sensation pleased him. A hug. Sand Boy's feet were cold on the marble so he slipped into a pair of cream knee-high socks. "Damn, son." He admired his reflection. "You're dripped up."

The ice cream melted as he tucked himself into the clouds of blanket and pillows. He poured vodka into vanilla cream and gulped it, bittersweet from the carton. Between sips he looked out the window onto the sand. He pictured Val in his spot. Val curled up in the sleeping bag by the sidewalk. Val shitting between cars.

A noise downstairs pulled him out of his daydream. Someone was trying to get in.

Someone made it in.

"Hello?" A voice called from below.

CHAPTER 18
TRASH MONSTER

Daily Horoscope: Aquarius:
When they call you too blunt get sharp.
Innovation makes everyone uncomfortable.

The Rat went out at dawn when the best garbage hunting went down. While Val slept, he crept out from under the sheets, slid down the bed, and crawled through a crack in the wall which led outside to the fire escape. He leapt from one metal stair to the next as if lifted by theater strings. Once safely on the sidewalk, he followed the smell of sweet garbage to get where he needed to be. Glittering trash pyramids lined the streets of New York City. Watch the black bags and they dance. Hot plastic rat disco. Who says Donna Summer doesn't blast from the slimy leftovers? Who says broken glass won't spin like a disco ball? It's Studio 54 with no guest list, anyone with fur in the game has a shot. Just put up a fight for the right spot.

Sure, there was some social order. Neighborhoods shape rodents like residents. Are you private school or juvie? Caviar or crack? Locked parks or broken-in cars?

Tribeca was the best, on all sides. Still, he had to play rough to score. Nothing hardcore, just some nibbles, a slap with his tail, a scratch here and there, you give some you get some, he's had a piece bitten from his ear. He came across this rat with a scar across her back; the hardest chick in the bag; and traded her a pizza crust for a prize he held in his jaw like a ball gag.

By the time he scuttled into the Roxy room drool dripped from his chin.

"Where were you?" Val yelled at him from the toilet.

He dashed to the bathroom, dropped the gift on the tiles and proudly pushed it with his nose so it rolled to her feet. She held the milky blue marble like a joint roach. It was slick with saliva and stank of garbage. Still seated, she reached toward the sink and ran it under warm water. Once rinsed, she wiped it with toilet paper. "Thank you, baby. I needed a good luck charm." She winked at him and his ears turned pink. That's how rats blush when they're excited or embarrassed. You can look it up.

"What are you up to today?" she asked. "I'm hanging out with hot poets, wanna tag along?" The Rat shook his head. "I read an Alex Dimitrov poem that broke my heart this morning. It was about Paris, blowjobs and drugs. You'd love it. Ugh, sometimes I think I should write poetry? Maybe it would be easier to get published. What do you think?" The Rat bit his nails.

Food was delivered to the room. She drank coffee and left the rest to him while getting dressed. "I never know what to wear with these girls. They're always sickening, they make me feel like some sad, old librarian." The Rat tilted his head. "Not because of how they treat me, not at all. They're *girls' girls,* the epitome. It's just, it's hard to explain, that nuanced female friendship shit, it's honestly easier to navigate when there's obvious resentment and competition, you know?" He blinked at her. "Maybe I should finally get around to reading that Elena Ferrante bitch, I think she explains it."

He finished half the food and looked to her before eating more.

"Oh, that's all for you, baby, I'm eating out." She posed in front of the mirror in a leather dress. "What do we think? With the leopard coat? Am I giving Kate Moss?" He sat on the room service tray, staring. "Or am I more Patsy Stone?" His back was arched, and his legs stretched in front of him, like a human. "Whatever, I'm late."

Val put the marble in her purse, making sure he saw. "Don't wait up!" He waved his tail at her. The door slamming shut always startled him, like a slap on the ass to a baby.

By the time she arrived at Lucien the girls were ducks in a row at the bar. She imagined they all arrived together, in a limousine, drinking champagne and laughing. They chose the spot, a cliché for New Yorkers longing for Europe. Lucien served the fantasy via buttery grub priced high and stiff drinks served icy. She squeezed into the last bar seat and listened to them scream over the noisy restaurant, and each other.

"Val's here! You bitch! Have a shot!"

Hanging with escorts suited her best because they were always dressed up and hanging around and had the best tea in town. Gossip was the only lasting currency, and women had all the stocks.

"What are we having? If I start with vodka, I'll have to stick to it…"

"Who cares what it is, we didn't pay for it!"

Val dabbled in sex work during college, but she was no businesswoman. She did cam girl gigs and pay-for-play arranged online, meanwhile her friends had regulars who took them to the Plaza. She changed sites, hoping to be more serious, and found a man from Dubai who said he'd be her sugar daddy.

On the first date he bought her a hundred-dollar dress from Zara. To her that was a luxury. She didn't think to take him to Prada. He paid her rent, which was eight hundred, and spent the night with her. He made her insert a vibrator he turned on by remote control when they were at dinner.

Her tolerance for bad men was high but she couldn't sit through bad dinners. After the Dubai guy she had a few more half-tries but had to admit she was missing something. Some instincts or boundaries. Common sense. Her friends who stuck with it were smart. Most of them were artists and writers, highly educated. The fact that sex work was still the best work a girl could get "these days" wasn't something she liked to linger on. With a drink she didn't have to.

Leonardo first found them at this restaurant, scouted like models at the mall. It became their thing, they'd get Lucien-drunk, hit Lucy's on Avenue A and end up at his apartment. Zooted till dawn and beyond. He published their first poems and dragged them into the world they weren't invited to.

Leonardo knew talent thrived anywhere, the more hostile the environment the rawer the writing. Better to pluck out genius at a KFC than an MFA. He was the only guy in the system who hated the system.

Not all poets are prostitutes, but all these prostitutes were poets. Vanessa (Leo, 32C) was one of two girls with naturals. The other was Val, who didn't count, since she was an A cup. Vanessa was a financial dom. She ruined men online. *Be my ATM machine* was her line. The Russian transplant had swollen lips, ass-length hair and a body men risked it all for—sometimes several times a day.

"I lost my Juul." Vanessa was frantic, digging through her purse and other people's purses. "I'll kill somebody."

"It's on the bar." Baby was an ex-pornstar who just moved back from LA. The Libra excelled there but missed being a Manhattan escort. Better money, less bullshit.

She resented the French manicures requested by producers. She wasn't basic (on the inside) but she booked basic roles. Girl Next Door Gets Creampied. Step-Sister Gives Head Over Homework. Sleeping Roommate Wakes Up To Pounding. Mormon Has Holes Examined By Priest While Future Husband Watches. The douching was killing her. She took Tea Tree Oil baths daily. She couldn't drive and got sick in the back of Ubers. When she had time off work she didn't want to go out. LA nightlife seemed soulless, and anyway she was a street girl, she needed to be on the streets. Fairfax and Melrose didn't cut it.

Val knew Baby hated LA because she lived in the Valley. Rookie mistake. That, and she didn't call her. Why hadn't she? She could have shown Baby everything. She'd have told Baby, LA is about the houses, the hills, the secrets. You can't just go out in public and bump into a party. You don't pound whiskey at a dive bar and wait for good luck. You've gotta give something up to get in. She'd keep it to herself now, only assholes dish out advice once it's no longer useful.

"Baby, your BBL looks major." Pearl was a downtown legend. The Capricorn knew she looked like a K-pop star. Her website advertised sessions for no less than 2k a pop. She was the hardest working poet in hoebiz.

"It's not a BBL. You need to gain weight for that."

"Oh you got retro implants. Same guy who got your boobs?"

"Yeah, the Rehab King."

"Legend. I've been considering it. Do you have a butt plug?"

"Well, you can't do it here. It's face in New York, boobs in Miami, ass in LA," Baby explained.

"Makes sense..." Vanessa sucked her Juul. "Like, you want a chic face, party tits and a bimbo butt."

Pearl said, "I can always tell when tits were done in New York."

"What, they're giving snob?" Baby pressed hers together.

The girls laughed. Val didn't know what to add, since she'd never had cosmetic surgery. "There's this rat living in my hotel room. I'm convinced it's Leonardo reincarnated."

Vanessa rolled her eyes. "Why would he be a rat?"

"He loved rats. They're smart, resourceful and underground, literally."

"Jesus, Val. Wait, you're coming to the memorial, right?"

"Are you really asking me? That's why I'm in town."

"You flew from LA just for the memorial?" Baby asked.

"Duh."

"Girl, you didn't fly out for Candy's wedding."

"Uhh,"

"You barely knew Leo."

"Well, he meant a lot to me."

"And Candy doesn't?"

Pearl cut in, not in the mood for a bar fight. "Who's down to eat crickets tonight?"

"Bitch stop trying to feed me bugs," Baby groaned.

"I just watched you guzzle piss on Brazzers."

"That's sterile!" Baby squealed.

"Where are we eating crickets?" Vanessa blew vapor at them.

"For the millionth time, Flaminco's. My boyfriend's spot? It was just written up in *The Cut*, hellooo."

"My bad, I'm brain-dead without my Juul."

"You're literally vaping it!"

"I've been dying to try Flaminco's." Val lied, she

hadn't heard of it, but she wanted to stay on their good side.

"You'll love it."

"Who all is coming?"

"Us, Amelia, that hot writer Joe and his bro."

"No way? I'd let him smash." Vanessa said.

"You and everyone." Pearl sighed.

"Leonardo loved Joe." Val pouted. "He was gonna publish us both. And Amelia, you mean the publicist, right? She was supposed to rep us. I'm kind of relieved I won't have to work with her, honestly, I think she hates me. She would have sabotaged my publicity."

"Amelia doesn't hate you, she's just a cunt." Pearl advised.

"She probably hates you." Baby grinned.

"And yeah, huge cunt."

"So why is she invited everywhere?"

"Cunt is a vibe." Vanessa snapped her fingers at the bartender.

The sun dropped as they walked to Flaminco's. Tourists, locals, commuters and bums stopped in their tracks to watch them. The gang wore platform Pleasers, Ostrich boas, crystal headpieces, vintage furs and dresses with zero opacity. Pearl complained about a client who wants threesomes with sex dolls. Vanessa said they're coming for our jobs and Val tried making a point on the ethics of artificial intelligence but lost her train of thought. Baby begged them to let her stop at McDonald's because she Googled Flaminco's menu and hated it. They all stood in line. Pearl got annoyed and said we gotta go. Baby said go ahead I'll meet y'all there but then she didn't.

Flaminco's was sleek and severe, packed with young people acting old and old people acting young. Pearl had reserved a long table by the kitchen, where Amelia, Joe and his bro were already seated. Amelia, classic Gemini, had on a gray hoodie with a beanie pulled over her head. Her face was plain and free of makeup, her greasy hair was pulled into a low pony and she wore brand-less jeans. The dull look caused terror. Her lack of effort made the other girls feel silly. Teetering in their heels like toddlers, creating a breeze when blinking with mink lashes, sitting awkwardly to avoid nip slips and camel toes while accommodating cleavage and whale tails. As they entered Amelia pulled her beanie off to flaunt bland authority.

"Sorry we're late," lied Pearl. "Traffic."

"You girls were at Lucien." Amelia snorted. "The owner texted me. Next time let me know, you can sit at my table."

"Wait, you were there? We didn't see you."

"No, I mean, *my table*, it's always mine."

"Oh, sick?"

"Yeah, I get my mail delivered there."

"Blimey." Joe spoke in faux-British slang though he was born in Nevada and never left the country. Imagine Madonna in the early 00s, though at least she had the excuse of being married to Guy Ritchie. He insisted it was a "style" rather than an accent. As if all writers choose their cultural identity. His buzz cut revealed floppy ears which made him more handsome. Men profit from their flaws. His nose leaned to the left and his eyes had a mean gleam. He was forever rolling a cigarette that never made its way into his mouth, which was busy talking shit or kissing someone's girlfriend.

His bro's name was Ben, but nobody remembered that. He was only known through Joe. Several years ago, he moved to the city to be a musician but ended up working at a bowling alley. He was planning his move home without telling anyone. A year from then people would think to ask where he's been but wouldn't know how to reach him.

"What's kicking?" The Chef appeared from the

kitchen, hugged Pearl from behind and lifted her chin for a kiss. The Chef was in love with Pearl since high school. They reconnected at a Bushwick rave when he pulled her out of a K-hole. He knew it was fate. Over breakfast he revealed his identity to her but she said she didn't remember him because she forgot high school. He asked how that was possible.

She said, "You can choose to forget whatever you want. If you don't remember, it never happened."

He asked the table if anyone has allergies or restrictions.

Val said, "I don't eat meat."

The Chef said not even fish? Not even fish. The Chef said not even bugs? Especially not bugs. Amelia butted in, why did you come here then? No worries, assured The Chef, I got you. He asked can I get you all started with drinks? Val ordered a bottle of Vermentino di Sardegna. The Chef asked that's for the table? No she said that's for me.

Vanessa slid from her stool. "I'm doing a bump so I don't pig out, I've got another dinner after. If anyone wants..."

"Me!" Val stood up. "You coming, Pearl?"

"I don't do blow anymore. It shoots into my third eye."

As Vanessa cut lines on the counter Val studied their reflections. Women love going to the bathroom together so they can compare their bodies in the mirror. You can't be sure how fat your ass is until you see it next to an ass you know the fatness of. Like when men photograph their cocks next to Snickers for scale. Once they cleared the lines, Val took a picture of them posing and posted it with the caption, "Russians invented glamour but Croatians invented hangovers."

Slivers of fish were served raw in shells that didn't host those fish when they were living. That detail seemed rude to Val. She was given a skewer of green peppers and olives in spicy oil. The others drank margaritas while Val sipped her wine. She felt a headache coming on, a really brutal one behind her eyes. She thought of her great-uncle in Montenegro, how he turned yellow before he died.

Despite being warned, Val was scandalized by the fried crickets. "The future is meat for rich people and insects for everybody else."

Joe tossed one in his mouth.

"And where do we fit in?" Amelia crunched.

"Fiscally rich, morally bankrupt." Said Pearl, plucking an antenna.

The Chef made Val a white bean soup which paired well with the wine she was halfway through. She was sat next to Ben, who ate quietly. She found him cute and hoped she'd get lucky. If a guy would do it for her she could feel it in the pit of her stomach.

Attraction was a sort of nausea. They made small talk. He said he's a drummer so she asked if he knew Caleb, as if all drummers have a group chat or something. He'd never heard of Caleb or his band. She'd never heard of Ben's either. He asked what she does and she said I'm an author. "That's cool." Said Ben.

Amelia intervened, "Influencers stay getting book deals."

"I'm not an influencer," Val snapped. "I'm famous *because* of my writing."

"When you got *Instagram*-famous," Amelia clarified, "your book wasn't out yet."

"But I'd written it. And it was optioned for film already—" She trailed off when she saw everyone staring. She knew it would be smart to shut up but she gulped her wine and went on. "Sure, I sold some books to my *Hollywood Coyotes* following. But I never 'influenced' them to buy anything else. I don't even post coyote content anymore!" *Crickets*. "My blue checkmark came from the book."

Amelia grinned. "Okay."

Val tried picking up where she left off with Ben but he lost interest. The next course arrived. Grotesque cuts of pig served with sauce. The Chef put the severed head in the center of the table so his tortured eyes stared at her. The Pig looked devastated. He watched the others eat his body parts. *It wasn't me,* she told him telepathically. *But you're complicit,* he replied.

She refilled her glass. The Chef forgot her vegetarian course. She packed her plate with bread. Nobody paid attention to her but The Pig. Her bottle was nearly empty by then, so when she closed her eyes to avoid his, her head would spin.

Amelia covered her mouth with her hand as she chewed and asked, "Joe, who else have you sent your book to?"

"I can't be arsed."

"Are you crazy?"

"I'm unsigned innit."

"The news is out. Anyone who knows Leonardo's legacy would kill to publish his protégée."

Protégée? Val thought. *Come on.*

"I'm gutted without Leo."

"Joe." Amelia grabbed his face. "Talk to me, I'm here to help." Her hand rested on his shoulder.

"You taking the piss?"

She chuckled. "Are you free Wednesday? I'll set up some meetings." Her free hand got a phone out.

"That's proper nice." He blushed. "I reckoned to ride my bike cross country on Wednesday but I can do it Thursday."

The nerve of these two, she thought. Why pretend she was less of a writer than him? He'd never even been published before. She was writing for magazines when he was just learning to jerk off. Leonardo had been her editor, too. She had just as much claim to his legacy.

"Leonardo told me a lot about you both, I was looking

forward to working with you, Amelia." Her slurring barely covered the bullshit. Amelia said nothing, so she continued, "I don't know what to do with my book, either. I mean, it's my second, but I'm unsigned, I didn't need an agent when I had Leonardo."

Amelia grimaced, then turned to Joe. "Isn't this pig delicious?"

"Real good nosh."

When she realized what just happened and that everybody witnessed it, she stood up and marched to the bathroom and sat on the toilet seat. Then she took The Rat's marble out of her bag and began to cry. After a moment Vanessa barged in. "Honey, don't take it personal, she's just jealous. She's dying to write a book."

"Well, that can't be it," she sobbed. "Because Joe wrote a book and she doesn't hate him. She's going to help him! And she iced me out. Did you see that? How she ignored me in front of everyone?"

"Are you stupid?" Vanessa squatted on the floor in front of her, so she could make eye contact. "She wants to fuck him."

"I don't get why she has to be mean." She sniffled.

"She was born with that mean face. It leads her."

"Well, that's not our fault. She could wear makeup."

Vanessa laughed. "It's not our fault she doesn't wear makeup. You ready to get back out there? What's in your hand?"

Val rubbed the marble. "It's a gift from Leonardo."

"Is it a crystal?" Vanessa took it from her and held it up. "Jesus, what a sicko."

"Sicko?"

"Leonardo gave you this?" She pushed it back into Val's hand.

"Kind of, yeah. It's just a marble."

"Val, no." She stood up and straightened her skirt. "That's someone's glass eye."

CHAPTER 19
GANGSTER GAME

The Man stepped inside and closed the door behind him. "You here, girl?"

Sand Boy didn't want a fight. He had a weak jaw, missing teeth and a twice broken nose. Throwing a punch took a lot out of him. It was probably the chick's boyfriend. Who knew when he'd leave? If he hid under the bed he might be stuck all night. He was just delirious enough to put on an act. With a grunt he threw off the blanket and hopped out of bed.

"Hello?" Sand Boy called out, as he tip-toed downstairs.

Good thing I came strapped, The Man thought. Val didn't say someone was home. The bitch usually got it, she always came to his car alone and if he met her at a party she'd walk down a block. She never tried introducing him to friends. Didn't give his number out. You can't be too careful. He took her ring out of his pocket, put it on a table and turned to leave, when he saw a blue blur.

"Hey, I'm house-sitting for..." He realized he didn't know her name. "My friend. I'm Brandon." He held out his hand. "And you are?"

The Man studied Brandon. Something about the

boy was off, not the dress, but an edge, like he'd been through it. It could be nothing, lots of rich kids had that going for them. Ketamine, and whatnot. "I'm leaving."

Sketchy snack. Brandon thought, looking up at him. *Don't act suspicious...what would a house-sitting friend ask of a friend of a friend?* "So soon? Can I offer you something? Her fridge is stocked with drinks."

The man hadn't stopped in hours. He had to piss. It wouldn't kill anyone if he took a break with a fruity friend of a cokehead. "Yeah, why not." He followed Brandon to the kitchen. "I'm Carlton."

"Would you like a drink, Carlton?"

"Just water, I'm driving." He drummed the countertop. "So how do you know Val? And where's the bathroom?

"Oh, Valee, right. We're neighbors."

Brandon only knew of the one upstairs, which held evidence of his reality, that pile of soiled clothes. "I just got here, I think it's that door to the left."

Carlton searched for the restroom. Brandon poured water for him and a glass of prosecco for himself. The bubbly was flat, Val had opened it that night she met her lawyer. He poured it into the sink and opted for a beer, which he opened with his teeth. An old habit, or a skill, really, not to be wasted.

Brandon was feeling it. Hosting parties used to be his thing, he'd have the gang over after a street session, skating between cars, bums, old ladies, whatever, risking their lives. A bunch of forties and no girlfriends in sight. There was nothing better. Those days they were kings.

Val's house was no rat pack rager, but the vibes were good, the sun was setting, that beer drank smooth and his guest seemed cool. Only music was missing. He spotted a turntable and a stack of records in a corner between two cacti. Her collection of jazz vinyl surprised him. Skip James lured Carlton out of the can. Brandon worried jazz would taint the mood, but that only happened with people who couldn't handle melancholy. He could see Carlton had plenty.

"So what do you do?" Brandon asked and immediately hated himself for asking. He used to joke, back when he partied, the best answer to that question, *what do you do*, is, "crack." Why would he ask that? He would only get asked in return.

"Sales. You?"

"Nothing, really."

That made sense, thought Carlton. Only rich boys dressed like that, looked that way, didn't take care of themselves, because they knew they could go to the hospital or buy a new suit any day.

"I love this song," Brandon said. "Wanna dance?"

"With you?" Carlton choked on water.

"Why not?"

CHAPTER 20
PLAYING HOOKEY

The check came to one grand, split six ways was one sixty plus tips. "Fuckin hell, mate, I'm skint," said Joe, sifting through his *quid*.

Pearl only made Val pay a hundred. "Because you didn't eat shit." Val said that's nice but then everyone else has to pay more. As they should, Pearl shrugged. Espressos were on the house. Val wondered why they had to pay at all if Pearl was fucking The Chef. They'd eat for free if this were a Balkan spot and instead of espresso they'd get rakija. Instead of Amelia there would be a land mine in her seat which would be less stressful to sit across from and easier to talk to.

After coffee everyone rushed off to their respective appointments and apartments. Joe was "pissed and knackered." Val smoked and Vanessa vaped outside as she called an Uber.

"Can't we party?" Val begged.

"I've got a date."

"I know, but after. I can stay up." She would do anything for another bump but knew it would be rude to ask on the sidewalk.

"The memorial is tomorrow, we should chill tonight."

"Leo would have wanted us to show up hungover

and hideous. He'd want us to stay up all night and not even change clothes."

"No, girl. He'd want us to arrive stunning and fresh as roses and then get totally demolished *at* his memorial. Cry off all our makeup. The works."

"I'll probably spend the whole night in the bathroom."

"Doing lines?"

"Hiding. I'm dreading half the guest list. Will Zach be there?" *Dior Homme…*

"Which one? I don't remember men's names." She rolled her eyes.

Val laughed, knowing Vanessa was dead serious. "You know, my ex, the edge lord, he's got that gross podcast."

"Oh, that one. Yeah, obviously he'll be there. He's like, lit scene royalty."

"You're joking," Val scoffed. "He's a fraud, he plagiarized his thesis. Did you know that?"

"Everyone knows that."

"Have you read his work? He's a misogynist."

"His old stuff, maybe, but he's grown a lot since then."

"I wouldn't know, I muted his name."

"Slay." She sucked her vape. "I guess it's hard to stay in the loop over there. New York is its own world. Remember? If you don't live here, you don't exist."

"Yeah, well, y'all don't exist for anyone in LA."

"YeAh, WeLl!" She mocked. "Nobody cares about LA, no offense. Anyway, he's become like, a Prose Podcasting Art Critiquing Paris Reviewing Rock Star. He's got this college girlfriend and MFA groupies."

"That's gross."

Vanessa's black car pulled up. "Be a good girl." They hugged. "See you tomorrow, I'll be wearing a veil!" Vanessa stepped into her seat like a movie star. She shut the door and rolled down the window. Vapor spilled from it and filled the street as she zipped away.

Val made a call. "Can you sleep over tonight?"

"I'm working," Ace traced the swirl of a snail shell with clear nail polish.

"We can raid my minibar."

"Basic minibar like crackers and Bud Lite or luxurious minibar like condoms and phone chargers?"

"Oh, they've got hardware, software, champagne flavored gummy bears and nothing for less than ten dollars."

Twenty minutes later Ace arrived at The Django in Smurfs pajamas and a white thermal. "What, I thought this was a sleepover?" They squeezed into a booth during the late set. Val ordered them martinis and macaroni and cheese because she feared Ace might literally be starving to death.

"I love this place." She stuck a macaroni on each finger of the fork. "It's my favorite."

"You never took me here."

She shrugged. "We were too broke to come here in college."

"I'm still too broke to go here."

Val nodded and acted as if her mouth were too full to speak. Ace continued. "But when did you start coming here?"

"When I worked for *GooGoo*...after college but before Caleb."

"Oh, I guess I wouldn't have known."

"Yeah, we weren't talking then."

Ace stabbed her leg with a fork under the table.

"OW!" she shrieked. "What the fuck?"

"What?" He laughed. She pinched his nipple and he shrieked louder. The band noticed their noise.

"Let's go before I'm banned."

. . .

They held the plates of food and cups of booze under their arms as they wobbled upstairs to her room. The staff didn't bother bothering them; they looked the sort of unhinged that either meant they were crazy enough to stab someone or rich enough to get away with it. Ace asked her to turn on the TV and she explained that she broke it the night she threw the remote in retaliation against Caleb's ex-bandmates. He said nice job and headed to the shower. The water ran while she searched her laptop for a series, eventually choosing *Absolutely Fabulous*, a show they used to stream illegally in the dorms.

Wheels on fire...

Ace screamed from the bathroom.

"Hey, everything OK?"

He ran out, naked and soaked. His enormous dick flopped around. The injustice of what he could offer. The Rat chased after him.

"He must be protective." Val giggled, letting him in her lap. "Ace is a friend, he is good." She explained, meeting her nose to his.

"That's the one you told me about? Or one of many others?" Ace slid under the covers.

"Just this baby boy." She put him in Ace's hands.

"Aweee, cute." The Rat let Ace scratch behind his ears. "What's his name?"

Val thought for a second then said, "Leo."

Ace accepted her delusions. He could be cruel about small stuff, but never held your darkness against you. He cherished the humanity; aware it was our best quality. Slurring, she unraveled her theory, the one she barely believed until the moment she heard herself say it out loud to the girls. Until then it had been bubbling in her subconscious, taking over her daydreams, until she couldn't deny it anymore. Once she told Ace, she was completely convinced that The Rat was Leonardo reincarnated. After his body was wheeled out of the room, this very room, she assumed, he was reborn as The Rat. Knowing Val would attend his memorial, knowing she'd made this painful pilgrimage for him, he greeted her upon arrival and has kept her company since.

"Alright, let's say that's true." Ace considered. "What does Leo want from you?"

"French fries, mostly."

Leo's eyes lit up when she said the words and he began sniffing vigorously. "Does he want you to tie up loose ends? People…rats…only stick around after death if they need vengeance." Ace continued.

"Happiness is the best revenge, isn't it?" She asked Leo, who deflated once he realized no fries were coming. He was lodged between them under the covers. Val kept her underwear on, to prevent any perversion induced by Ace's beauty. She wasn't sure Leo understood what they discussed but he seemed content to rest between warm bodies.

"I think revenge is the best revenge," corrected Ace.

"In that case, I should kill whoever gave him the bad dope."

"Do you know his plug?" Leo lay across Ace's neck like a scarf.

"Maybe. In the last picture taken of him, he was wearing this shirt I gave him. From my *Vanity Fair* photo shoot?"

"I don't know what you're talking about." He lied.

Asshole. "Come on, you know the pic, I'm naked in a blonde wig."

"Doesn't ring a bell, babe."

"I put that pic on my merch and sent a shirt to Leo when he was editing my novel."

"You have *merch*? What are you, twelve?"

"Yeah, listen, the night he died, he sent me a picture, to show me he was wearing it. And in the pic, he's with this guy, who used to write for *SICK* magazine. A drug columnist. He must know something."

"Do you know this *SICK* guy?"

"Yeah, I slept with him ages ago."

"Of course you did."

"It was a threesome with his girlfriend, who kind of pushed me into it. She was obsessed with having threesomes. She kept pulling all her friends into their bedroom. They were this iconic Williamsburg couple. She wrote about sex and he wrote about drugs. He fucked us on the rooftop of his building, against a fence, with a view of Manhattan."

Ace put Leo on his head. "Go find him."

"And then what?"

"Get the drugs that turned Leo into a rat."

Val laughed. "They didn't turn him into a rat, they killed him, and then he came back as a rat."

"You should take those same drugs and turn into a rat, too."

"That's brilliant."

"I know."

"I mean, I know you're kidding, but it's actually brilliant."

"I'm not kidding." He twirled Leo's tail around his finger. Leo's eyes darted between them as they spoke about him as if he wasn't there.

"Do you know how to shoot up?"

Leo began to squirm, and jumped onto the pillows.

"I'm sure there's a YouTube tutorial."

She got up and grabbed her laptop—the piece of metal she should be using to write a new book, or push her latest work, which she was only using to watch porn—and placed it on the cuckold chair. Every hotel has one, in the corner, facing the bed, so husbands can watch their wives get fucked. Leo ran off the bed to the bathtub.

CHAPTER 21
ANY BUG CAN BE A BED BUG IF YOU LOVE IT HARD ENOUGH

"Nah," Carlton shook his head. "I'm not dancing with you."

"Bummer." Brandon twirled.

Carlton watched Brandon. He was awkward, lacked rhythm and seemed drunk. "I gotta get going."

Brandon said, "Fine, get up, then." He eyed Carlton's pants, which moved. "Oh, you already are."

"Huh?" He looked down at his body betraying him.

"It's cool if you have a boner."

"I don't have a boner." He adjusted his boner. Brandon kept dancing, moving back toward Carlton. Carlton crossed and uncrossed his legs.

Brandon swayed toward him and put a hand on his knee.

"What are you doing?"

"Shhhhh." Brandon put his fingers on Carlton's mouth.

Carlton could kill Brandon with his bare hands. He trained to fight as a kid and could have gone pro but went to jail instead. On the inside he fought more, Rikers was like Gladiator camp. The kid aggravated him, but he held back. He didn't want to leave a crime scene at Val's or have to clean one up.

"Yo, stop. I'm serious."

Brandon lifted his hand, bent to meet his gaze and gasped. "Sanpaku eyes."

"Sanwhat?"

"Three whites!" Ah, shit. That exclamation point meant the booze hit. Like his mother, he was a lightweight. Drinks made him chatty, like her too. "So, regular eyes show white only on the sides but Sanpaku eyes show white under or above. Eyes like yours mean a doomed fate. Princess Diana had eyes like that."

"What are you getting at?"

His drunk game was whack, trying to pick up by threatening destiny, hurting feelings and shit. He backtracked. "It's all good, you got the glamorous version."

"Oh, yeah? What's the other version?" Carlton rolled his ruined eyes.

"Psycho killer, qu'est-ce que c'est? *Fa-fa-fa-fa, fa-fa-fa-fa-fa*." He swayed. "If you've got white *above*, you're in trouble. That's psychopath shit. Charles Manson had eyes like that. Him and my math teacher."

"Wow," Carlton said. "I'm out." Serial killer talk killed his boner. He got up.

"What's so important?"

"I got a delivery." Carlton jiggled his car keys.

"Ah." Brandon looked outside, noticed the Mustang. "That's your ride? I've seen you here lots."

"Yeah, well I'm Val's friend."

"No." He smirked, "You're her plug."

Carlton headed to the door and Brandon grabbed his shoulder. "Can I cop?"

"You got cash?" Carlton looked at Brandon's hand on his shoulder.

Brandon squeezed Carlton's shoulder. "Front me?"

"Hell no." Being touched by him sent some kind of

shock through his body, like those acupuncture electrocutions.

"Trade you for it?" Brandon took Carlton's head in his hands and kissed him.

Against all sense Carlton let him. His lips were soft like a girl's.

They kissed again and then Carlton pulled away, against chemistry. "I don't do this." He reminded himself.

"Don't worry, I'll take care of you." Brandon grabbed Carlton by the hand and in that moment, Carlton abandoned control of his own body. Brandon led him toward the bedroom. Following him up the stairs, watching his skinny body move in that dress, Carlton tried accessing his sanity. *What are you doing? Stop it.* He heard his own voice and ignored it. *Stop it!* He saw himself from above, moving toward ruin, against all logic. Like seeing an accident take place in slow motion and realizing only after the fire starts you were the one driving. The voice was powerless; only his heart was in charge now, followed by his dick. He let Brandon undress him and put him in bed. Brandon didn't get any, he knew Carlton wasn't ready. He got off on getting Carlton off. He got off on changing lives. Brandon didn't date gay men.

"Scratch my head?" Brandon begged on the sweaty sheets, after hours of hard work that melted into a flash.

"Don't you want blow?" Carlton reached out and ran his fingers through his hair.

His whole body was soft, warm jelly.

He laughed. "I was kidding. I haven't slept in days."

"Why haven't you slept?" Suddenly Carlton cared for this boy's well-being.

"Long story. Maybe I'll tell you tomorrow."

Brandon recalled his puddle of clothes in the bathroom. He realized he should probably get up and move them, before he forgets, before Carlton sees, but Carlton started snoring already. And his arm was so heavy over Brandon's waist. And finally, after days of agony, he could feel the dream world approaching. He shut his eyes and dove into the void.

Somewhere in Malibu, a cokehead stayed awake in a sober rage. He tore his house apart trying to find "leftover coke." But we all know there's no such thing.

CHAPTER 22
YOU CAN'T GO HOME YOU CAN'T STAY HERE

Daily Horoscope: Sagittarius:
Getting what you want
doesn't feel as good as wanting it.
Even fire needs air.

Ace was gone when she woke up and in his place was a poem scribbled on the Roxy notepad.

Dear Val,
Thanks for the macaroni,
which you mostly ate.
Sorry to leave, I hate goodbyes,
and have a Grindr date.
One day we'll be together, our destiny.
You and me, two rats in the city.
Your best and most attractive friend,
Ace

She ripped out the page and stuck it inside her copy of *Hollywood Babylon*, which rested on the glass eye in her purse. Leo snored on his pillow. "Good morning baby boy." She petted him between his eyes as he opened them. Her fingers traced the bridge of his nose, scratched behind his ears, massaged his back and rubbed his belly. When parted, his dark fur exposed pink skin, silky and warm. She would die for him. "Are you hungry?"

Yes, he pushed his head into her palm. "I'll order pancakes." He stretched as she called room service, then curled back up on the pillow. He'd squeeze in more sleep before breakfast. The previous night was a blur that left her feeling heavy. The pressure of purpose. She opened her laptop and the tutorial on how to shoot up started up. Purpose took the form of a DM. She found the *SICK* writer's Instagram profile. It said Follow Back. Her message shot into his primary inbox.

"Sup Hank long time since the rooftop ;) can I ask you something?" She brought the sex up to startle him, to plant doubt in him. Men were "scared" now, rightfully so. They feared that deep down they didn't know, couldn't remember, were unable to tell the difference between right and wrong. Someone bringing up sex from ten years ago felt like the FBI kicking down your door. Did I forget to take the weed out of my bag before going through airport security? Did she say no? Did she mean it? Cold sweat. Not for what you did to her but what she can do to you, now.

She sent the question and headed to the bathroom but she didn't feel like showering. She wanted to keep Ace's scent on her. She slipped on ugly white underwear, tube socks and a black tracksuit. Then she brushed her teeth, washed her face, slathered on lip gloss and sunscreen. She had a big night ahead, which called for fake lashes, caked foundation, baked powder, an overdrawn lip line and eyeliner reaching her ears. She'd let her skin rest while it could.

"Yo what's up?" He replied.

"So, this is kind of random but you know how the last picture taken of Leonardo was with you?"

"What picture?"

Knock, knock, knock...

She forgot to stop the delivery boy at the door. He came inside and saw Leo sprawled out on the pillow.

"Is that a rat?" he asked, deadpan.

"No," she answered.

"That's a rat."

Leo held his pose, frozen.

"No," she insisted. "It's a micro purse."

The boy was lost. She watched him calculate if this was worth the trouble. Was this her fault or theirs? Is it a pet policy or maintenance issue? Would she take pictures of The Rat and sue? Has he been living under a rock and missing fashion cues?

She signed the check with an extra fat tip, hoping it would silence him, then she grabbed the tray and pushed him out. "That was close." She set the tray by Leo. "Next time I'll be more careful. Kudos on staying still." He dragged a pancake off the plate and onto the blanket. He nibbled the edges, eating from the outside in. She sat on the pillow next to his and grabbed a pancake with her left hand, folding it like a slice of pizza.

With her right hand she scrolled photos and landed on the last one Leonardo sent her. She'd stared at it a hundred times, through ninety-nine tears. He looked on edge and up to no good. His smile held a secret. The pic was taken by Hank. Only Val knew this and she only knew because his reflection lurked in a black window. She sent him the proof.

He typed and stopped. She finished her pancake. He typed and stopped. She gulped coffee and burned her tongue. He typed and stopped. Leo lapped milk. He replied.

"What do you need?"

"Can I come over?"

"I'm tired."

"No cardio, just conversation."

"You can write me here."

"Are you sure? Evidence???"

When he sent his address she groaned. "One oh eight. Jesus. I must run, Leo. Finish breakfast at your leisure but please, *please* hide from the cleaning lady. I'll be back before the memorial to dress up." He sat back, belly up, full of dough. She stepped into her boots. "You'll help me pick out a look. I need to serve tonight. I need to kill." She could swear this time he waved at her with his paw.

Maps said a taxi would take one minute less (39) than the subway (40) so she splurged. She would have taken a taxi anyway but this way she felt good about it.

Uptown may as well be Iceland; she was used to taking thirty or more to get anywhere in LA but the rules were different here. Who had that kind of time in New York? People cut friendships over a borough change. She rarely went above 14th Street. Girls like her only left downtown for penthouse sex parties or when a friend was left alone in a suite when their John went to work.

When she stepped onto the street, she felt too bare, maybe she should have brushed her hair, there's only so much sunglasses can do. Her reflection shot her a look from a storefront window, and it made her sick. Fuck it, she wasn't going there to fuck him. Not in that way, at least. His place was by the park. New Yorkers hang around parks and Los Angelinos hang out in parked cars. It's true, if you ever find yourself walking in LA, you'll notice many parked cars on the street have people inside them, sitting, watching their phones, eating from Styrofoam, or just killing time.

Practically the only free thing you can do in that city is sit in a parked car—once you get out, it's a different story. A car parked without a human inside of it can mean parking tickets and a human walking without a car around them can mean so many bills and receipts. A human and car combo, that's ideal, it's purgatory.

In the elevator she turned her back to the mirror to spare herself from her vanity. The doors opened directly into his loft. Hank's place was a hoarder's paradise, with no surface to rest her purse on. The spot was packed but not filthy, kind of like a professor's office, a smart man's mess, bursting with information. If someone were to arrange his trash on a great wall, it would reveal answers to questions that could fix the world.

Hank was in boxers and a tank, and she had a weakness for men with tattooed legs, especially if the legs were muscular, like his on full display. He skated, and had style, meaning, in the straight boy world, that he wore Palace. He was attractive enough to make pussies pump without making homeboys jealous.

He shook her hand hello as if his dick had never met her mouth. She regretted not dressing up or at least showering. They could have had fun on his trash if she didn't look like garbage. She thanked him for seeing her. He said I had no choice. They stood in the kitchen, with nowhere to sit. He didn't offer her anything to drink. She took the hint and got to the point. "Can you tell me what went down that night?"

"He called me up and said he was in my neighborhood and that he just scored and wanted to come over." As he talked, his eyes quickly shot back and forth, as if he were rewinding a tape, sorting through his memories, to get the facts straight.

"So, you didn't help him score?"

"He got it, I had nothing to do with it."

"Why'd he come over then?"

"To test it."

"Test it?"

"I've got a lab here, you know, I study this stuff."

"Oh, really? I didn't know." She did. Everyone knew

he had a TV show. He skyrocketed to legitimacy while all the girls who wrote better than him sank into obscurity.

"I don't know why he bothered testing it. I told him it was a bad batch, dirty, hardly any dope in it. He didn't care, he was so intent on it. Said he hadn't scored in years, wanted to celebrate, a special occasion, good news, or something."

"Yeah," Val sighed. "He was going to start his own publishing company, nobody knew this. Me and that other kid were going to be his debut titles."

"Oh, yeah? What was he doing with the other company?"

"Leaving. His partner screwed him out of money. You know that big movie deal they got with Apple TV? They made three million off it, the author got one million, his partner got two million and Leonardo got nothing."

"That's fucked up."

"Yeah, so in response, he was like, fuck this, and decided to start his own company. It was on the down-low, nobody knew about it yet. And it was a risky thing to sign on to, as an author. If it were anyone else, I would have said no. But he's a genius you know?"

"Yeah, everyone knows he's a genius." Hank was jittery, shuffling things around, like he wanted her out.

"It was gonna be huge. Earlier that day, before he met up with you, he told me he had great news from investors. So that's why he wanted to celebrate, I guess."

"Yeah, he couldn't be talked out of it." He crossed his arms tight and sighed.

"You could have thrown it away though...or made him do it here? So you could call an ambulance or use Narcan or something?"

"He wanted to go to his hotel, rock star style." He shrugged. "People make their own choices."

"You know what's crazy? The only scene he made me edit heavily in my new book was a heroin overdose scene. Because I had written that this kid OD's and someone shoots him with Narcan, but Leonardo was like, when your book takes place, Narcan wasn't around yet. So he made me change it, so that the kid's friends put him in a cold bath. Isn't that insane when you think about it?"

Hank blinked at her.

"So do you know where I could get it?"

"Get what?"

"The stuff Leonardo got."

"Why would you do that?"

"None of your business."

"I've got some here, from what I tested. You wanna keep it as a souvenir?" He laughed at her.

"I'd like to do it myself."

Snickering to himself, he disappeared into his lab. She wondered how he'd find something tiny in piles of crap but miraculously he reappeared moments later. Some hoarders were organized like hamsters.

"Don't make me regret this." He placed a tiny ball of tin foil into her palm.

"Did he tell you where he got it?"

"No but I recognized the baggie, it's from the bodega on the corner."

"What's on the baggie?"

"A middle finger."

She sat in the park and fingered the ball of dope in her pocket. The wind blew through her tracksuit. She was hungry. Children played nearby. A couple shared a bubble tea. Teenagers smoked weed behind a bush and the smell reminded her of LA. She dreaded going back, she had nothing to go back to. Her new book filled her with anxiety. She felt kidnapped by her own life. "Location scouting for my suicide," she tweeted.

Her email inbox was full of crap. Since arriving on the island, she'd lost six hundred Instagram followers. A couple of rats ran by as she fondled her pocket. *I wonder how little Leo is doing.* A smile formed on her face as she thought of him.

With a sudden burst of energy, she stood up and walked to the corner store. America's soul lives in bodegas run by immigrants. Balkan thugs peered through the glass at the Russian salad, which Russians call English salad. Croatians call it "Francuska Salata," or French salad. She loved it, like all Croatians do. Her mom would make it on New Year's Eve, like all Croatian moms. She'd spend all day cooking and cutting carrots, potatoes, pickles and eggs. She'd toss the cubed food with gobs of mayonnaise into a ceramic bowl she used once a year, only for that salad.

Val would sneak bites from the bowl while it cooled in the fridge. You aren't supposed to eat it warm. She'd double-dip the spoon into the mush and flatten it as much as possible and re-cover it in the tin foil but Mama always found out and freaked out because Val smashed her germs into the whole salad and ruined it for everyone.

Eventually Mama let her have a small bowl of the warm salad before cooling the big bowl for the rest of the family. Nobody made Francuska Salata like Mama. Store-bought Francuska Salata was for the desperate, people without mamas. This one looked terrible. Jelly mayonnaise and mushy vegetables, clearly frozen before they were cooked and chilled again. But she couldn't resist it, after all, she was desperate now. Without a mama.

"Sorry, ma'am?" She sought the attention of the lady behind the register, slumped on a stool playing a game on her phone with the volume at maximum.

"Da." The lady replied. Her phone made explosion sounds.

"Can I have the Francuska—I mean, Russian salad?"

"Where you from?" she asked while playing.

"Zagreb. You?"

"Split."

More blasts.

"I was always a Hajduk Split fan, even though Zagreb is Dinamo, because my first boyfriend loved Hajduk. So that stuck with me. Plus the Bad Blue Boys are fascists. They always tried to beat on me for being a punk."

She shrugged. *Bang, Bang, Bang.*

"So can I have some?"

"No."

Bam, Bam, Bam.

"Šta?"

"It's no good." The boys came to the counter. The lady got up with a sigh and rang them up. She lost her game over cigarettes, Red Bull and Goldfish Crackers.

"She's right," said one of the thugs. "It's no good."

"It's poison," said another.

They wore tracksuits, like her. Unlike hers, theirs were knockoffs, with fake Adidas stripes. One had long black hair and the other had a shaved head. Both had scars, prison tattoos and attitudes. They looked like twins, either aged eighteen or thirty-eight.

"My body, my poison."

The lady shook her head as she scooped a lump of what claimed to be Russian salad into a Styrofoam cup. "Six dollars."

"Six dollars? That's insane."

"My store, my price."

"Jebiga." Val took her salad and followed the boys outside. They stood on the corner with their cigarettes.

"Can I bum a smoke?"

"They're menthols," the one with the hair said apologetically.

"Perfect." She grabbed one from the pack and let him light it. He used a Zippo lighter with a cap on it. The sound one of those makes in a man's hands was what she imagined high heels on a good pair of legs sound like for men. His knuckles were swollen and cracked but his fingernails were cut short and clean. Dirty boy with good hygiene. When he got close, he smelled like cabbage and rakija, like home. "Can I ask y'all a question?"

"Y'all? Where are you from?"

"I grew up in Appalachia, so I talk like a redneck. But I'm Balkan, like *y'all*." She emphasized for comedic value which they ignored.

"Who said we're Balkan?"

"You look like my grandfather." She blew smoke. "He's from Montenegro. The Appalachia of Yugoslavia."

"That's crazy." His grin revealed a chipped front tooth. Her kryptonite. "I'm Montenegrin." His ancestry was obvious. The wiry hair, ancient skull, black hole eyes.

"Since we're family, can I ask something?"

"Shoot."

"Know where I can score?"

His grin slammed shut. "Nah." An oyster guarding its pearl.

"Oh, come on. You seem cool."

"No dice lady."

"You don't know about any middle finger baggies?"

"What are you talking about."

"I'm no narc."

"What are you?" He held his cigarette between his thumb and forefinger, like a roach. He closed his eyes as he sucked in. When he blew out, he looked past her, squinting into the horizon, as if watching for enemies. Who taught boys to perform these gestures seared into the shared feminine psyche? Did he know what he was doing to her underwear?

"I'm a writer."

"Ah, my brother was a writer."

"What happened to him?"

The grin reappeared. "Ask him yourself."

The bald boy broke his silence. "I'm not a writer," he said. "I'm a poet."

"Have I read you anywhere?" she asked the idiotic question and felt ashamed.

She hated being asked that question. He would, too. Look at the poor guy, of course she hadn't read him anywhere.

"Maybe. I've been in *The New Yorker*, stuff like that."

Stuff like that? She gulped.

"It doesn't matter. Didn't change shit."

She'd never made it into *The New Yorker*. Was he fucking with her? He must be fucking with her. She was being prejudiced against her own people. Her brothers. Brate! Forgive me! Anyway, poetry was different. It didn't count.

"What's your name?" she asked so she could look him up.

"I'm Damien. That's Tomislav." No last name. Damn. Could she ask him to Google himself right in front of her? Maybe in a few minutes. "What's your name?"

"I'm Val."

"Bullshit. What's your real name?"

"Slavica. I took the middle and turned it around. I like that Val means wave, and these Americans don't know, they think it's some Hollywood name."

"Why didn't you take the middle and keep it as Lav? Lion?" They flicked their cigarettes.

"I'm more water than animal."

"We're going back to ours, wanna party?"

"I thought y'all don't party."

"I never said that."

She followed them further uptown.

CHAPTER 23
PANIC AT THE PEEP SHOW

> DAILY HOROSCOPE: PISCES:
> WHEN PLEASURE RULES YOUR LIFE,
> YOUR LIFE IS PAIN.

Brandon woke in an empty bed, blanket stuffed between his legs, two pillows under his head. He stretched like a cat and took a moment to place his coordinates.

Whenever he woke in a strange spot he heard the Talking Heads. *How did I get here? Carlton.* Water sprinkled on marble meaning he was in the shower meaning he was in the bathroom with Brandon's filthy clothes.

> DAILY HOROSCOPE: ARIES:
> DO YOU WANT YOUR TRUTH
> OR YOUR SANITY?

Carlton scrubbed the fault from his skin. Regret met inner peace. Another dimension tore open last night, he bit Eve's apple, took the red pill, came in another man's mouth. There was no going back.

"How's it hanging?" Brandon walked into the bathroom, kicking his clothes into the closet and closing the door. "You shut those special eyes of yours?" He'd thrown Val's slip back on, for Carlton's sake, so not to shock him with nakedness in the sober sunlight.

"Too long," he answered. "I missed a drop last night, gotta bust ass to Malibu."

"Come back after." Brandon watched him lather his body. He was ripped, clearly lifted and started young, but something about him seemed wonky. His strength was distributed unevenly, maybe because of too much time spent bent behind the wheel. Carlton hurt on the road; Brandon hurt on the streets.

"*Some* people have to work." He shut off the water and shot eyes at Brandon.

"Take a day off."

"I can't."

"Or what, you'll get canned?" he teased, handing him a towel.

"These fools count on me." He woke to a mountain of missed texts. Countless exclamation points. Cokeheads aren't loyal, you leave them spiraling dry one night and they'll find someone else by morning. Shit product, high price, no matter to them.

Response time and readiness were his most vital aspects. He worked from 3PM to 3AM usually. The deliveries rarely made sense logistically. There was no way to organize his drops, he was at their mercy. The only client who booked him in advance, with timing and location options for his convenience, was Val.

"Can we fake your death?"

"Shut up." Carlton wrapped the towel around his waist and gargled Val's mouthwash. He made eye contact with Brandon in the mirror behind him and blushed.

"Can I ride with? I'm a fun shotgun."

"Nah, man."

"I won't touch your radio." Brandon stood in front of the closet of horrors.

"You don't got shit to do?" He walked into the bedroom.

"I'm house-sitting." Brandon trailed him like a dog.

"Right." Carlton scanned the floor for his clothes and piled them into his arms. His jeans heavy with his gun.

"You want breakfast?"

"I don't do breakfast." He dressed quickly, modestly, facing the window.

"Well, I'm starving." Brandon jumped on the bed and lay on his side, head propped in his hand. "I'd hit Dogtown, their breakfast burritos rip." Brandon used to eat them regularly. A leggings girl fussed over him for weeks. She'd drop a burrito off before Pilates. He didn't have the heart to tell her he didn't eat meat. He'd leave the bacon in the sand for the birds. She stopped showing up a while ago, and that was alright, all his people came and went. "You ever had a Dogtown burrito?"

"Can't say I have."

"Rain check?"

Carlton tattooed Brandon's glorious image into his brain and solemnly declared, swore on his life, that he'd never see him again. "Sure."

CHAPTER 24
FAMILY AFFAIR

Their bleak apartment was spotless. Balkan sons and ex-cons know pride in maintained order. Only the rich live like animals. Messy bitches always have maids. She felt at home and at ease, she could have eaten off the floor or cut lines on the toilet seat. They sat around the kitchen table, touching feet. Tomislav poured plum rakija, neat.

"Živjeli, Slavica."

The liquor warmed her throat and soothed her soul. It tasted like Grandma's.

Every ex-Yugo grandma had two things in common: state-funded abortions and bootleg booze. She resolved that Tomislav would get it, if she had to choose. She could make out the shape of him under his tracksuit. She asked for a fork for her Russian salad. Damien handed her a spoon.

"I said fork."

"This is eaten with a spoon."

"Forks are more elegant." She even ate ice cream that way and it used to drive Caleb crazy.

"Budala." Tomislav gave her a fork.

The slop was rancid. The sour vegetables dissolved in her mouth. A bitter paste.

"Užas," she said, closing the cup and pushing it away.

"Tsk, tsk, tsk." Went Tomislav. "You going to waste that?"

"You better finish it." Added Damien.

"No way, brate." She shook her head.

"We don't waste food here." Tomislav pushed the cup back to her and refilled her shot glass. "Help it go down." They stared her down as she drank. Maybe she'd have them both. Her crotch was soaked. The Styrofoam squeaked as she opened the cup.

"Good girl." Barked Tomislav.

She salivated.

Ding, Dong.

"Who's that?" She asked, fork raised.

"Some friends." Damien got up to open the door. "I told you we're having a party." Three men piled in and the room temperature dropped ten degrees. All in ill-fitting suits, tight on the shoulders and knees. They were sniffling and grinding their teeth.

She rarely acknowledged or respected a bad feeling, convincing herself for years that "trusting your gut" was a concept she associated with the weak feminine, with pussies. She hated admitting to herself, in retrospect, that she knew something was coming, and chose to brush it off, as a dare to herself, against her gender. But when the bad feeling comes in threes it's hard to ignore.

"Well," she said, standing. "It was great meeting y'all, but I've got a memorial to get to and I need to go downtown and do HAM."

"Ham?"

"Hair and makeup, it takes me like two hours." She said proudly. They had no idea how she could beat her face into a completely different person, no idea they'd want to marry who she could be in two hours.

"But we came for you," said a suit. He put his hand on her shoulder and pushed her into her seat. His hand was the size of her face. She recalled when kids at school would say, "If your hand is bigger than your face you have cancer." So you'd put your hand in your face to check and the other kid slams it so you slap yourself.

He squeezed her jaw, and she pulled away. "You're lucky I'm not in makeup now because if you fucked it up, I'd stab you with this fork." The familiar fault lines cracked and seared into her body years ago had been waiting to erupt. And here it was, rumbling. She looked down at her cup.

"Russian salad?" he asked. "It's my favorite."

"It's everyone's favorite," she scoffed.

He grabbed the fork from her hand. "What you guys have no spoons?"

Damien tossed him one. He snickered with Tomislav. They watched the suit scoop a heaping spoonful into his mouth. "Hmm." He grunted. "Good."

That confirmed Val's suspicion that he was a psychopath.

"I'll put on a movie." Said another suit, plopping on the couch. He turned a porno on with full volume. She watched the men watch a girl get gang-banged on the big screen. Their eyes burned her back as she made her way to the bathroom. She shut the door, but he pushed it open before she could lock it.

"I gotta take a shit," she stammered.

"I'll watch." He locked the door behind him and pushed her toward the sink. He stank of Dior Sauvage. Oh, no, confirmed sex criminal.

"I'm not joking." Her voice shook.

He undid his belt. "Ej, mala. Suck my dick here or fuck those guys out there." In moments like these, which she found herself in often, which is relative to say, but it felt like it happened to her more often than to other women, or at least she hoped so, for their sake, in these moments, she couldn't help thinking of what the funniest thing to say would be. How funny her Tweets would be about the moment, a few months after the moment, when she'd had time to workshop the moment over brunch with other girls who have had similar moments. "Why not both?"

"Think I'm playing? I'll throw you to the dogs and they'll tear you apart."

"Dude, chill. Damien and Tomislav brought me here, they're cool."

"Get down, beba." He opened his fly and started stroking himself. "You should thank me; I'll be easy on you. And then you can go to your funeral."

"Memorial," she corrected him, dropping to her knees.

The better she blows the faster it goes. She couldn't help giving great head. Just because you're forced to do something doesn't mean you shouldn't put your heart in it. Like the janitor at her middle school. He mopped the floors every morning, whistling. "Hello, sunshine," he'd always say. If he could whistle while he mopped, she could do this.

She wondered if she were blowing the man who sold the bad dope. Leo would think it's hilarious. He'd tell her to put it in a book. He was more than an editor; he was a curator, a fire starter, he'd always tell her, "Give me danger!"

In her attempts to avenge him she ended up blowing his killer.

He'd say, Val, dealers don't kill people. He'd never blame somebody else for a thing like that. He had ethics. She couldn't believe he was underground. The suit grunted as he pushed her head into his hips. She took her middle finger and stuck it up his ass.

CHAPTER 25
MEXICAN STANDOFF IN MALIBU

On the Pacific Coast Highway, with waves sparkling on his left, hills to the right, cars ahead and more from behind, heaven above and hell beneath him, Carlton only saw Brandon, felt his hands and heard his moans. When he let himself take it all in: Brandon's eyes rolling into the back of his head in ecstasy, his smooth stomach and hairy legs, the scent of his neck, how he said Carlton's name, shocks jolted his gut and spread to his skull and made him feel faint and stupid. Sex flashbacks were a leading cause of car accidents. He told himself to concentrate on the road, but it morphed into Brandon's face when he slept, mouth open, forehead creased. He arrived at his destination with a painful boner.

Carlton rolled into the Malibu mansion, right where Miles Davis used to stay. It makes sense that when someone makes it, they want to get as far away as possible from the people who made it possible. Carlton had meant to do a drop there after leaving the ring at Val's. The client waited for him all night, texting Carlton while he kissed Brandon, smelled Brandon, touched Brandon. Carlton spoke his name out loud to himself as he walked to the door. "Brandon." It felt like a prayer.

The door was half open. The client's home, with panoramic views, direct beach access, midcentury furniture and marble imported from Italy, looked like it had survived a robbery. "You here, man?" Or a raid. "It's me."

Carlton walked into the living room, among flipped-over cushions, emptied drawers, objects scattered on the floor.

"Sorry about last night, I got held up." He looked around at the place, which felt spooky. Footsteps came from behind. The client snuck up and put him in a choke hold, a weak piggy-back.

"Yo, what the fuck!" said Carlton, holding the client on his back.

"Get out, devil." The client huffed in his ear.

"Bro." Carlton slid out of the choke with a juvenile Judo move and tossed him onto the sofa. "Chill."

His eyes were crazed. "You can't hook a guy then leave him dry. I spent the night searching and I found something from a past life…and you know what? It's clear now. I understand everything."

"Calm down. I got you a free ball for your trouble." Carlton reached for his pocket.

"No! I'm done with you! I'm done with that!"

"Oh, yeah? What are you on now?"

"None of your business." His face was rabid.

"Alright dude, look, I had an emergency at home."

"Never ruin an apology with an excuse."

"My bad."

"Do you know who said that?"

"No."

"Guess."

"Machine Gun Kelly."

"Benjamin Franklin said that!" he shrieked.

"I was kidding." Carlton sighed.

"Whatever. Get out, devil, I'm done with you."

He was pissing him off but couldn't afford to lose him. "How can I make it up to you?"

"You're evil, you ruin lives, how do you sleep at night?"

"Listen, I'll just leave the stuff here, it's a gift." He put the bag on the coffee table and the client moved backward.

"Get out or I'll shoot." He pulled out a revolver and held it up.

Carlton laughed. He was harmless, a roid head with too much time on his hands. He probably only bought the piece because Joe Rogan told him to.

"I'm serious." He shook the revolver toward Carlton. "I'll shoot you, devil."

Now he was angry. "Stop calling me that." He reached for his Glock.

"You're what's wrong with the world. You wanna play?" He held up his gun. "You don't own me anymore." He waved it around.

"Listen, you NFT pushing, incel reddit posting, crypto losing motherfucker."

The client cocked his revolver.

Carlton squeezed his handle and aimed at his face. "I'm warning you."

The client pulled his trigger. Carlton leapt back and shot.

The client's head emptied itself on the sofa. His gun wasn't loaded.

Carlton passed through the living room onto the balcony and ran down the wooden stairs. He walked through the sand and straight to the water and threw his gun into the waves. With his phone he did the same. Nobody was around. The client had a private beach. Nobody should have a private beach.

CHAPTER 26
DIRTY BUSINESS

She grabbed the Russian salad on her way out of Balkan jail.

"Jebem vam mater," she said.

The open sky was humiliating. Her phone said she had two hours to get downtown, do HAM, feed Leo and get to the memorial.

From inside a taxi, she called the Roxy Hotel to order room service for Leo. As she did, her phone shook with texts. Vanessa's name took over her screen like pop-up ads in the early days of websites.

She hung up the call and read.

"Hey babe, I need you to pick up some devastating candles for the ceremony! You know the white ones, in glass tubes? Can you get like, a shitload? From that witchy shop in East Village."

Are you kidding me, bitch? I don't even live here, why do I have to do it?

"Yeah, no problem!"

Should she go to the Roxy first to change and then get the candles on the way to the memorial? Or get the candles first and then change without that task hanging over her head? She made the wrong choice and told the driver the new address.

It took an hour to get to the East Village.

Ding, dong. The door swung open to the smell of lavender. A petite blonde arranged flowers on a table holding spells. "Beautiful day!" She sang.

The shopgirl wasn't witchy enough to work there. Her hair was the wrong kind of blonde; not bleach-fried, but aluminum-foiled honey. Her nails were round almonds when they should be pointy coffins or bitten bloody.

"I need candles for a memorial. Those long white ones in glass?"

"We've just got some new scented candles in. This one smells like matcha!" She held a green wax blob to her face and inhaled.

"It's for a memorial," Val reminded her.

"What's that?"

"Are you serious?" Val pushed past her and rummaged through piles of candles. The ones she chose cost twelve dollars each. She packed them into a cardboard box that was heavy to hold. The Russian salad cup sat on top. The girl rang Val up with one hand while dusting tarot decks with a feather duster with the other.

"Can you pull me a card before I go?" Val asked.

"I couldn't possibly."

"What's your rate? I can pay."

"No, I mean, I don't know how to use these or whatever."

"And you work here? Jesus. OK. I'll read it, you just pull it." She requested, clutching the box on her hip like an infant.

"How?"

"I ask a question, and you think about me, and pull a card. Easy."

The girl shuffled the cards clumsily. "Fine. What's your question?"

Will I live another day? Does it matter? Has my life been wasted? Is there any hope or mercy? Did I take every wrong road? Has my own heart turned against me? Am I destined for tragedy? Why can't I feel joy, only agony? "Um, I don't know…I guess, how will tonight go?"

"Okay." The fake-ass witch closed her eyes and pulled The Tower card.

"Fucking great," Val huffed.

"What? It's not a good one?" She flipped the card over in her hands, inspecting it.

"It's the worst."

"I'm sorry, it's my bad."

"No. It's me, tripping up the stairs in stilettos eternally."

"But you don't really believe in this crap, do you?"

Out on the street, hunting for taxis, she asked people for the time. That's the most off-putting question you can ask these days, when even the unhoused have phones. She held her box out to them, as if to say, you see, my hands are busy. A teenager broke the news that she only had half an hour to go, so no time to change. She'd look like trash at the event she'd spent nights awake planning looks in her head for. Only a full face and painful shoes complement a tortured heart, and she'd show up in a tracksuit.

Val cursed the universe and the sky started dripping.

She walked in the right direction hoping to flag a cab. The clouds couldn't contain their leak. At once an ocean dropped from above.

She hid under a bodega awning, careful to not trample the rats by her feet. They reminded her of Leo. That bellboy was a narc, what if he kicked Leo out and she never saw him again? She'd have to leave him anyway. Did she even think about that? What had been her plan? To fly him to LA? *"This is my emotional support street rat, we're from New York City, you wouldn't understand."*

. . .

It took forty minutes to walk to KGB bar, a fitting place for Leonardo's goodbye party, since he used to host readings there. Val had never attended these events, but he'd told her all about them. She'd daydreamed of being part of the debauchery one day. Not like this, no way.

By the time she arrived her tracksuit had soaked up the rain and weighed a ton—at least it was black. The killer dope in her pocket was protected in foil. *The murderer at the memorial,* she thought, dropping the Russian salad on the floor. Now that's comedy! Leonardo would have asked her to "set up" that joke from the beginning. It's too late for that now. Life is a manuscript you can't edit. The roughest draft.

On all fours, she arranged the candles in a circle, by the altar at the door. Framed photographs of Leonardo had been placed there by others, along with flowers, books, notes and novelty gifts hinting at inside jokes. She felt envious of those who had longer, closer, more profound friendships with Leonardo. Now the inner circle would exchange anecdotes, competing for who misses him most. People piled in past her.

"Does anybody have a lighter? Anyone?" she asked, and they ignored her until a manicured hand gave her a pack of Lucien matches.

The hand led to an arm, which led to Amelia, who wore archive Margiela, had a full face of makeup and looked spectacular. There was something particularly offensive to Val about women who usually dressed themselves down, put no effort into their appearance as a sign of superiority, and then put themselves together exceedingly well when the occasion called for it. As if to say to her, I could be like you if I wanted to, but I choose not to because I have better shit to do.

"What are you doing?" Amelia grinned.

"I'm putting these candles here…Vanessa told me to."

"Ok…well, don't be late. The room will fill up fast."

I got here before you. "Yeah, thanks for the tip, I'll rush."

Val lit the candles quickly. By the time she came up, it was true, everybody was there already, and they were all dressed exceptionally. Men wore smoking jackets and tuxedos, women were in dark furs, long gloves and lacy veils, surely taking cues from Vanessa in some group chat Val wasn't invited to.

*At least nobody will recognize me…*she hoped, shivering in her wet tracksuit. Following the heat, she approached the main room, where the literary in-crowd all stood, sat, gossiped, spat and snorted off keys.

Amelia shot a look at the lady sitting on the stool at the door. She held a list. Val was on it but that didn't matter. "It's all full in this room, you'll need to go upstairs."

"But nobody's upstairs," she protested.

"You'll be the first." Amelia stood behind the list lady, affirming her authority.

The air grew colder as she climbed the creaky staircase. No heat reached that floor. At least there was a bar, with a lonesome bartender, who made her a vodka on ice which she brought to a table. Alone she listened to laughter floating up from the main room. *They're laughing at me I bet. Or worse, they aren't.* She checked Twitter and saw that a minute before, Amelia had tweeted, "Some people bring out the gatekeeper in me."

On the bright side, she told herself, *up here I'm safe, I won't see Him…Dior Homme. The man who raped me and went on to become a literary legend.* She laughed out loud. Who was she kidding? She'd love to see him! She craved a reunion. Only he really saw her; he'd always looked at her like she was something to eat. In her darkest, most depraved moments, only he took her in, understood and forgave her. The first man who made her unashamed of her body. She'd lay on the bed with her legs spread, and he'd just watch. "You belong to me," he'd say, and he was right. Betrayal can only taint so much and only if you let it. Days after a session she could recall a moment and lose her balance in the street. "You're my dog." He rewired her brain and then he stomped on it.

Val ordered another drink at the upstairs bar and took it down to the bathroom, hoping someone had copped. On the way there she noticed the door lady was gone, probably having a line in the toilet herself. This was her shot into the good room, into redemption. She slid inside unnoticed and tucked herself into the crowd.

She walked up to various groups, trying to insert herself into the conversations. But mostly she just listened, invisible. They pretended she wasn't there. Was she?

"Women are biologically useless after thirty-seven."

The conversations swirled around her, incoherently.

"When you're unattractive you have no choice but to force sex on women."

"I've graduated from counting calories to counting words."

"If we nickel and dimed each other every time we needed each other's prescription medicine, we'd be no better than animals."

"My first book was too relatable and that's a shame. I want my work to be so specific it's alienating."

"I want to stop hating myself, but I want to continue to indulge in the behaviors that lead to me hating myself. I want to be different but don't want to change."

Val wondered if she sounded like these people when she talked. Was this really the literary elite? No wonder nobody read books anymore…

"I have to be this good-looking because my personality sucks."

"I did buy your book, I swear, but that same night I ended up at a Goth rave in DTLA and vomited all over the side of an Uber on my way home and had to use the ripped-out pages to clean the car."

"I just quit smoking, and I still crave the smoke, so this guy was walking in front of me on the sidewalk and he was smoking a Marlboro light, my favorite, and his smoke was trailing behind him as he walked, and I was like, yum, yes! So I started following the smoke, it was hitting the spot. And after a few blocks, this guy turns around, he's like, why are you following me? How do you explain to someone you aren't following them, you're following their cigarette smoke? I guess I was following him, though, essentially. Anyway, we ended up fucking in the Dunkin' bathroom."

"I want my next book to be like those TikTok videos that say, you can't possibly expect anything that happens in this video. And it's some old Chinese man in the countryside cooking hooves or something, and I want it to feel that surprising, but that once you read it everything made sense, like, it couldn't have possibly been any other way. Does that make sense?"

"The thing about me is I make shitty choices, but I stand by all of them."

"Yeah, I would send shit-stained panties in the mail for money, but I don't have shit-stained panties laying around and I'm honestly not sure how to make them."

"When a relationship ends it's like a bad finale to a good show.

Like, the finale of Game of Thrones. A bad ending makes all the time you invested in it, enjoying it, seem wasted. But why? When you look back on your happy memories with your husband and think, well that's sad, those two idiots didn't know it would end in divorce. That doesn't take away what they had then. Don't do that to that version of yourself. Let her live on there. Just because your life will end in death, does that make all your experiences leading up to death pointless?"

"I don't have any regrets because I know that no matter what I do, there is heartbreak either way."

"I'll blurb your book if you let me eat your ass."

"No fire sign should have a driver's license."

"I don't remember drinking it, I shouldn't have to pay for it."

"As a person she's nice but her aura is toxic."

"Poets are supposed to die poor."

"I was flirting with him heavy on WhatsApp, he's Italian, so, they love that app, anyway, we were so into each other, until I stupidly changed my icon, I was drunk one night and just decided to change it, no big deal, right? But you know, people really get used to that icon, it sends pleasure waves to their brain, it hits a mental G-spot. But I changed mine, like a fucking idiot, and I changed it to something "funny," a dog in a wig. A fucking dog wearing a fucking wig! An ugly dog, in an ugly wig. Jesus. I did it in the middle of our flirt-fest, and I swear to you, he got colder toward me after I changed my icon. And I don't blame him! It's like, what the fuck was I thinking? His brain, his balls, must have felt like, why is this dog sending you horny voice memos? Who is this bitch, literally? This can't be who you were getting hard for all these months, is it? So anyway. Now I'm trying to win him back with this new icon, I

can't change it back to what I once had, not now, obviously. So now I'm stuck with this dog in a wig. For as long as it takes."

"I used to Google am I a bad person? Now I Google how to live with being a bad person."

"Lots of women stay in bad relationships to show their goodness, their suffering. That's the big scam, that women are supposed to be good. We do insane things to show how good we are."

"It's easy to be generous with someone else's ass."

"You can write THE END on anything and end it."

"Wouldn't it be funny if when a deadline comes you actually die."

"I spilled wine all over my bed and I don't know what's more sad, to sleep in a wet bed or sleep sober."

"Did you hear Amelia got Leonardo's protégée a 200k book deal?"

"I get so bored of being the only fun at a party that I play games with myself."

"Once I stuck toilet paper into my underwear and had it trailing behind me on the ground. I waited for someone to tell me but nobody did. They thought it was Vetements."

"Male authors will eat your ass but won't blurb your book."

"I'm writing a book with a male lead, so boys are tricked into reading it. By the time they're hooked I'll devastate them, with a pegging gone wrong and big musical ending."

"He learned Japanese just to read Murakami in its original language. And he said the translations are better."

"I think I'll fire my therapist because I'm still crying every day, it's like I'm leaking, maybe I just need a plumber."

"People ruin their entire lives for a good plotline."

"She had a whole ass divorce just to write a book about it, you'd think the book would at least be good."

They're talking about me, about my book! Val snapped out of her eavesdropping coma. Who said the last part, about her book? She zoomed in and out, searching. And there he was, across the bar. Dior Homme. That man from her past who got away with murder. How long had he been staring?

Val held up her cup. "Cheers." She mouthed silently. He shot her a nasty look.

That look still made her feel useless, useful only to him. Her stomach flipped and she looked at the floor. Watching her feet, she pushed through the crowd in no direction. *There's a napkin, some spilled beer, a cherry, who would waste a cherry, an empty plastic baggie, it's been flipped inside out, licked clean, good for them, sticky stuff, oh, nice shoes, here we are,* when she saw a free spot, she plopped on a couch. Spinning, with her eyes closed, she smelled it. The Dior Homme scent. Then saw it all, his red-lit bedroom, the movie posters on his wall, a tiny old-fashioned television playing music videos on a loop and his hands reaching toward her throat. A wave of nostalgia for the most painful time in her life pulled her down in a rip tide.

"I read your book," he said in her ear.

"So did everyone," she gargled.

She'd pictured this moment a million times, but the revenge fantasy version of her was sober, and rather than being sloppily slumped on a sofa, she was standing upright, having some sort of career-win, perhaps, a big public display of success, an acceptance speech, preferably. In the fantasy, she wore something stunning, worth her rent, the rent she used to pay when she paid rent, not a soaked-through tracksuit. The fact that in this moment, the real moment, she looked and felt so pitiful, killed her. But hey, he liked her dirty. He'd seen her covered in spit, piss and blood. "Your true self," he'd say in those moments. Anytime she'd show up showered and made-up he'd mess it all up in minutes. Did he like the book? Could he find himself between the lines?

"What are you doing here?" he asked.

What was strange wasn't how strange this felt, but how comfortable she was. "What are *you* doing here?"

"I was friends with Leo." He sat closer and took her hand in his.

"Yeah, me too." She didn't flinch, his touch was comforting. She wanted to rest her head in his armpit and cry. She wanted to tell him about Caleb, her sad career, loneliness, Leo, the Montenegrins, "He was gonna publish my next book."

"Really, kiddo? I didn't know that."

"Nobody does. Nobody will, now." She did it, she put her head on his shoulder and sighed.

"Hey, why so glum?"

"Don't ask." How glad she was that he was asking!

"So you're divorced now, or what?"

"Kind of." Her lap was wet again. You could call it resilience. "Listen, do you have any blow or anything?" She met his eyes, pleading.

"No, but I got something else you like." He lifted her by the armpits and led her to the toilet.

As she followed him through the room, she considered the version of herself that was angry all those years, the one who thought she earned some sort of payback for her pain. She'd rehearsed telling him many things many times, usually right after cumming about him. Something along the lines of, *you're not the only man who did that to me, you know. You're just the only one I feel bad about. Or, I wasn't really yours, all that time, I was lying, it was a performance, I was bored.*

Sometimes she imagined a slap, a kick in the nuts, some kind of pain. But her imagination was limited when it came to violence against others. Daydreams were one thing but, in his presence, she stood no chance. She just wanted him to want her again. What she thought was revenge had been honor, she'd only been preserving the memory by dedicating her life to fighting it.

Pressed close in the bathroom stall their bodies knew the old moves. He held her mouth open and spat.

"Let me hear it."

She begged for his cock the way he taught her to in college.

"Louder."

"There's other people here," she whispered.

"I don't care." He put his hand down her tracksuit and shoved his fingers so far inside her, tears bled onto her cheeks. "Take it." He said, and then, shocked by something, he pulled away. "Kid, what the fuck?" Repulsion tainted his voice.

"What?" She panted. "Why'd you stop?"

"You've got a condom inside you." He held it in her face. It was hard to recognize; it didn't even resemble a condom anymore, just a scrunched-up piece of yellowish plastic.

"Oh…gross." She grabbed the thing and threw it into the toilet. "I'm…I'm so sorry. But. Ha! Thanks for finding it?" She looked at her feet. "I'm so sorry."

"Do you even know when it's from?"

Boston in Berlin, inside her for days. "Um."

"Jesus, kid, you're a mess."

"Good thing I use condoms though." She pulled her

pants back up, forcing laughter as her humanity cracked around her.

He left her in the stall, slamming the door behind him, then washed his hands aggressively in the sink, cursing to himself. She stood over the toilet, waiting for him to leave. The condom swirled as she flushed. Declaring something your rock-bottom moment implies you can't get any lower but she knew by then it was delusional to presume.

Before he left the bathroom, he said, "You're disgusting."

In the main room, Leonardo's husband had finished making a speech. She'd just missed it by a minute. *You flew all the way to New York for this memorial, for this moment, for this speech. And you missed it because you were being fingered in the bathroom like a pathetic whore.*

When she approached the main room, she saw everybody in tears, embracing and applauding. She spotted Vanessa in her veil, clapping with hands clasped in Madonna prayer. Her and the girls sat in a velvet corner being gorgeous. Dior Homme headed toward them, to spill what just happened. She could start a fire, end it all for everyone.

She ran to the exit, where her candles burned around her Francuska Salata, deserted in a puddle. "Let's get out of here." She told it. "I'll bring you to Leo, he must be starving."

The rain had stopped by then and the clouds were parted in that way they do only when you're a teenager in love, or tripping on acid, or being greeted by God reaching down through streaks of sunlight.

In the cab his voice rang in her head.

YOU'RE DISGUSTING

CHAPTER 27
LOVE IS THE DRUG

"Yo I fucked up." Carlton's car smoked the driveway, and he let himself in. Brandon was laying on the couch watching *Scooby-Doo on Zombie Island*, the best film in the franchise, an undisputed classic.

"What do you mean?" He sat up and patted the spot next to him. His face was so puffy, so innocent and childlike. Carlton couldn't believe he'd left an angel here that morning, to do what he did.

"Don't ask." Carlton sat down next to him and grabbed a pillow.

"You can't just say something like that and tell me not to ask, you tease." Brandon rubbed his back.

Carlton screamed into the pillow.

"Don't freak, man." Brandon put his arm around him and tugged him close.

He looked up with red eyes. "Is that *Scooby-Doo on Zombie Island*?"

"Yeah, it's goated. 1998 was a great year for cinema. And music. *Celebrity Skin* came out that year. I actually prefer Hole to Nirvana."

Scooby-Doo groaned on screen and Carlton groaned with him.

"Sorry, I'm rambling. What's up with you, baby?"

"I can't tell you." He buried his face in his hands.

"Boo, you whore. I'll share my secret , you share yours."

"I know yours. I saw your clothes in the bathroom."

"Ok, damn."

"You clean up nice." He looked up and smirked.

Brandon hid his grin behind a hand. "Yeah, well, wanna know how I got here?"

"No need to."

"It'll make you feel better about whatever you're going through."

"Doubt it."

"Trust."

"Try me." Carlton watched the cartoon as he listened.

"So, I was a gifted kid. I know everyone says that about themselves."

"Do people say that?"

"Yeah, everyone says they were gifted kids."

"Maybe the kids you grew up with."

"Well anyway, I really was gifted. I did well in school, I studied literature, I did an MFA."

"What's MFA stand for?"

"Mother Fucking Assholes! No idea. They're these writing programs. Hard to get into. Did you ever watch *GIRLS*?"

"Nah, man."

"Damn, so, we're having a binge ASAP. Alright, well, you're stuck with this group of writers and can't leave until you critique and discipline and beat each other down to the pulp to get the good shit out. The writers in my program were pieces of shit. I hated them. It was mutual."

"Sounds like prison."

"Way worse. So one day, they were critiquing my work, and I just couldn't take any more. This bitch was like, you don't know how to write women, blah blah blah, and I was so close to knocking her out. But I don't hit girls."

"You sound way too proud of that."

"Shut up, listen, so, I swear to God, just to keep from smacking the cunt, I stood up, I left all my shit on the table and walked out. And I walked off campus. And then I kept walking. I decided it would be poetic to walk all the way to the beach. That's what a real writer would do."

"How far were you?"

"Far, man. Iowa."

"What? Yo, why didn't you walk to the East Coast at least?"

"The East Coast blows."

"Say less."

"I didn't walk the whole way, I mean, I hitchhiked and hopped trains and shit. I got here, went to Dogtown, hung around, the rest is history."

"Do you write still?"

"Fuck that. Nobody reads."

Carlton laughed.

"Did I make you feel better?"

"No, but you made me forget for a second."

"Ok, tell me your shit now."

"I can't have you knowing."

"I'm no rat!"

"You're stressing me out. Can I just hide out here a minute?"

"I got you. Stay as long as you want. Or until Val comes back."

"Are you her friend for real?"

"Nah, but she really did offer her place."

"She left her spot to a homeless kid."

"Yeah, the bitch is crazy."

He laughed. "She's alright."

"Lay down with me." Brandon pushed his skinny

body into the back of the couch and made room for Carlton.

"Maybe just for a second." Carlton squeezed in with him so that they faced each other. Brandon's pupils were so dilated they looked black. Dragon eyes stretching to take in more of what they love. Carlton closed his and began to cry. If they'd met when he was younger, he could've been a different person. If he'd stayed this morning, they could still be. Shaggy screamed on TV.

"Hey, from the heart, I dig you so much, it hurts me to see you hurt. Please tell me what's happening."

"I don't want to lay it on you."

"I feel it already, man, don't hold back."

"It's heavy shit." He kept his eyes closed and squinted; forehead strained with memories.

"I thought I was clear."

"Clear from?"

"Look, there's only two ways out of the dope house and that's death or prison. I was lucky. Some cat gave me a package when I was just a kid, and I got caught up in a sweep, and I took the fall. So I got respect at Rikers for not ratting, and I had cats there I fucked with on the streets, so they had my back, to an extent. But it's not fun, man. I can't go back." He began shaking at the memory.

"Why would you? What happened?" Now Brandon was freaking out, but he was still careful not to say, *what did you do.*

"Things went sideways with a client."

"Do you want to elaborate, baby?"

"No."

"Ok. Well, your clients, that shit, do you gotta do it?"

"What choice I got? I've been around, it's all the same."

"Maybe you could do something else."

"Like what?"

Brandon smiled. "Nothing."

"Nothing, like you?" Carlton smiled too.

Brandon kissed him. "Nothing, with me."

"I'd like that." Carlton pulled him in closer and closed his eyes. Brandon stroked his hair as he wept. Some days are longer than others. Actions echo through space. On screen, zombies rose from the swamp.

CHAPTER 28
THE LAST LAUGH

Back in her hotel room, she peeled off her wet tracksuit. All she could do was lay in bed and text The Man. "Thanks for always being kind to me, it always meant a lot. In some ways, you were the best part of LA. I know that's lame to say. Anyway, here's a link to my new book, parts of you are in it. If you hate it don't tell me. Love, Val." The message bounced inside a fish's belly.

"Holy shit. What? No, way." Thinking The Man blocked her, feeling that rejection, realizing what he meant to her, that he was her favorite person in the city she called home, that she had nothing to come home to, aside from Sand Boy, and even he hated her, was too much to take.

"Leo?" she called out frantically. "Leo, help me."

She collapsed on the carpet and curled into a ball. He ran over to her and crawled up her legs, over her back and into her hair. "I'm so sorry." She sobbed. "I'm so toxic around you." He licked her neck. "I may be pregnant, you know. Or have hepatitis or herpes or syphilis. But it won't matter anyway, not at this point."

Leo's belly grumbled in her ear.

He wouldn't touch the Russian salad so she opened him a bag of chips and a tin of cookies and put the salad in the mini fridge, so it could rot in peace, with dignity. She'd grown fond of that poor dish. They had so much in common.

She ran a bath as Leo sat on the tub, sprinkled in potato chip crumbs. She wanted to tell Leo what just happened, how she had the most humiliating moment of her life with the man who had already humiliated her, how she missed any potentially positive moment the memorial could offer, how instead of redemption or closure she only ripped open her healing wounds. She should have stayed in LA. She should have never been born! He watched her soak like a gargoyle, her face twisted, mouth gaping, howling for relief. She didn't even make sounds, just silent, empty screams.

When the water turned cold she stood up, determined and serene.

She tore a page from the Roxy notepad and penned a suicide note. *A writer lives differently from people who don't write, but a writer dies like anybody.*

The tutorial on how to shoot up had been streamed in vain, there was no time to cop a kit. In one hand she held Leo and in the other the drugs. He was scrambling, scratching her, making strange squeaks. "Calm the fuck down, dude, this is none of your business." He looked as if he were crying real tears, but she knew she was only projecting.

Naked under the blankets, which felt thin and stiff, she unwrapped the foil with shivering hands and placed the dope dot on her tongue. Next to the bed sat a flat Diet Coke and she gulped it all down. Leo was scratching her mouth and her face. "Take whatever you want when I'm gone," she said, covering his head in kisses. "My dearest comrade, I'll miss you so much." He kept scratching, fighting for her life. "You can eat my face, if that's what you're getting at. Just don't mourn me, go live your life, you have so much to look forward to."

At that he seemed to give up and decided on cuddling while he could. She laid back on the pillow, with Leo on her face, panting feverishly. She ignored his despair and closed her eyes, thinking of mornings, muffins, making Mama drive her the "long way" to school because she didn't want to go, not ever. The only good thing that ever happened to her in that building was finding a copy of *Weetzie Bat* in the sink of the gym bathroom, which changed her life. The book, not the bathroom.

Matching Leo's frantic breaths, she shot off into nothing.

CHAPTER 29
NEPTUNE THE FISH

The transparent monster slithered across the sand, desperate for dust. The only mercy nature showed to his kind was the darkness. Bottom dweller, they called him. Yeah, it's grim down there, it's so dark you can't use that word. Dark is too light a word to describe what this is. Maybe the Scandinavians have a word for it, or the Siberians, but Neptune the fish wouldn't know, there's no time to read when the weight of the world rests on your fins. Those who say it's lonely at the top have never been to the bottom. They haven't survived the absence of everything all at once. You can roast his gnarly ass for being hideous, demonic, grotesque, mangled and cursed by God, but have you seen how he glides? Don't you care at all about elegance?

He was born under a good sign. The sun shone extra bright that day and though those rays couldn't reach him, he felt it. The truth doesn't need you to know that it's there. Light doesn't care if you acknowledge its existence. Being a deep dweller means being born wise, destined to love what can't love you back. You take the loss because it's your duty, pain is your purpose. And Neptune the fish felt the earth break before the humans could. And what could he say, but, hold on.

. . .

Val woke up spooked in a pool of cold sweat. Her body felt tender and rotten, and her vision blurred as she opened her eyes. She turned over to find a turd on her suicide note.

"Way to leave a bad review, dude," she moaned.

Leo smiled from inside a stiletto, smug at her survival. He uncurled himself and ran to her, even though he was angry. He wasn't sure he could ever forgive what she attempted, right in front of him. As if his feelings didn't matter simply because they were contained inside rodent packaging. In one hand she held him to her face, letting him lick the sweat from her forehead.

With the other hand she flicked his little shit onto the floor, held the note out and read aloud what she'd written, hoping it was brilliant, that it would have changed the trajectory of her career, if she really had passed and someone had found it.

It said: "If only I may have, at death, a friend's hand laid upon my forehead." A poem called "An Old Song" by Tomaž Šalamun.

"I couldn't even come up with my own suicide note, Leo. That's so embarrassing. If there ever was a sign I better start writing again this it or I really will have to kill myself."

She could only start fresh after mourning. She needed refuge, a place to connect with her past, all that was lost and never even happened. She didn't need to write an original suicide note. What she needed to write was an email to the Leonardo Foundation. He'd taught writing workshops there over the years, and hosted writing retreats. Now word was they'd turn the villa into a proper charity, helping writers of his legacy. Val looked at Leo the Rat, and knew this was her only hope. At Leonardo's villa, she could write herself back to sanity. Or at least another novel…

. . .

Hey! It's Val…I don't know if you remember me. You were in the background of one of my Zoom calls with Leonardo once. Also, I saw you at his memorial, from across the room, but you were deep in conversation, and I was honestly too drunk and embarrassed to say hi. Great outfit! Were those Rick Owens boots? Anyway…

I'm so lost without Leonardo. I know we all are, but I'm, like, plagiarized suicide note sort of lost. I'm emailing you to ask for help, like a Nigerian scammer, like an old man running for President. If I stay in New York or LA for one more minute, it will be the end of me, not to mention my "art." If you can call it that. I need to reconnect with THE MUSE (red wine, European men…) and get my shit together. I KNOW your Foundation is the answer. And I'd be so good there, I swear. I'm a classic "personality hire," the town jester, the joker in the pack, I'll sing for my supper and wash the dishes after.

I admit, there weren't any plans for me to stay at the villa yet. And I just missed the deadline for residency submissions. But I'm begging you, on my hands and knees (I can attach a picture, upon request). Open your doors to me and save a stray animal in need.

. . .

As the email swooshed out of her outbox, the time turned 11:11. "Make a wish." She told Leo. He did.

She opened Instagram, hoping for a dopamine hit, but her feed was a flood of bad news. "Is this for real?" She exclaimed. Shaky videos showed apocalyptic destruction. Traffic jams pushed forward by the Tsunami. Walk of Fame stars cracked in half. "The Big One" finally showed up on set. Hollywood got her big finale. "Damn, FOMO…" she joked, stunned, still dope numb. "You know, I think I'll send a follow-up email, adding that I probably just lost my home."

She opened Google Flights and tried navigating a wet screen. As she scrolled, her finger slipped. A teardrop had plopped from above, but it wasn't hers. She petted Leo, who was sitting on her shoulder, like a parrot, knowing they'd soon say farewell."

Skaters know that an empty pool is cooler than a full one.

Brandon woke to a wall of water and reached for Carlton. "Baby—"

END

if time is real
then tell me how
your last touch
lasts eternity
I'm stranded
in our hour
shipwrecked
by your wave
eternally

CHAPTER 30
THE HEART HEALS LIKE CEMENT

"The villa is haunted, but your casetta shouldn't be. This is where Leonardo used to sleep. The only thing is, it can get a little musty, like any old castle."

Marta led Val to the stone house attached to a castle, down the hill from the villa. When she opened the door Val was smacked in the face by nostalgia.

"I like the smell." She stepped inside and took a breath. "It's a safe stink, it smells like hiding from bombs as a baby."

"Just be sure to open the windows every day." Marta said automatically, used to Americans being easily offended by European decadence.

"I wasn't hiding in a castle, obviously, it was a basement. Castles and basements are equally rank, if you think about it." She looked around and shivered. "You sure this isn't haunted?"

"I don't think so. Pietro, our priest, he threw Holy water in every corner. Also in the villa. But by the time he did it there, it was too late."

"Ah, like Botox. Works best when it's preventative. What kind of haunting are we talking?"

"Nothing crazy, but sometimes, during the residencies, the writers will be in bed, and we'll all hear someone's moving furniture downstairs, or dancing. Sometimes it sounds like a party. And the next morning, we'll talk over breakfast and realize nobody left their rooms all night."

"Spooky."

"Yeah. We call them the *fantasme incazzate*. Anyway, you'll be here alone, so you'll know. If you hear something, it's not another person. I'll give you a couple local numbers in case you have a mental breakdown and need a getaway car." She winked.

Val went pale.

"I'm joking! But also, you're kind of meant to go crazy here. That's the point, right? To lose your mind writing."

"Yes, I have a new plan, to go mad, like Dostoevsky."

"That's the spirit."

"Spirits."

Leonardo's villa usually hosted groups of writers together, in intervals, for residencies. They made an exception for Val. She came during dead season, so she'd be solo. The villa was an hour away from Syracuse, perched atop a high hill overlooking a tiny town with the essentials for survival.

"Speaking of spirits, has anyone seen Leo?"

"Brad swears he saw a glimpse of him in the bathroom mirror."

"Lucky him."

"I'll let you get settled." Marta turned and stomped up the hill. She was a Spanish author and Leo's best friend. They met years ago at a writing workshop. She said Leonardo wrote the best story of the group, something about a man who did too much MDMA one night, and while screaming to some song, his mouth got stuck open, lock-jaw, it wouldn't budge, but he was so high he kept partying, with his fixed face like the *Scream* ghost. Leo always wrote the best stories, but he preferred being an editor because writing required too much discipline, he said. Since his passing, Marta and Leonardo's husband maintained the foundation in his name. Marta replied to Val's email after the memorial, wondering where she had gone that night. It turns out, after she ran to her room to try and off herself, there had been a world-rocking afterparty at Pearl's apartment.

"I was hoping we'd meet, because I was always there when Leo would be on the phone with you, discussing your book and things. I feel like I know you already." She invited Val there to work on the book Leo meant to publish, or a new one, or whatever she wished. Val had nowhere to go and no reason to live, so she got a one-way plane ticket.

Leo the Rat stayed behind. He wasn't cut out for the slow European life. Before check-out she ordered one last tray of room service, with both pancakes and French fries, and wrote him a love letter. Unlike her suicide note, this wasn't plagiarized. By her signature she left her phone number, in case he needed it. Doing so didn't feel ridiculous, and he understood. Leaving him behind felt wrong but they both knew there was no other way. Some love isn't sustainable, some love isn't meant to be kept in a routine, some love hits and runs and leaves you with a forever headache, a hangover you'll never get rid of, one you learn to live with and cherish, for the pain reminds you of joy.

She felt a rush of fear as she watched Marta disappear behind the trees.

The casetta was one room, with a sink, mini-fridge, toilet, shower, bed, sofa, desk, chair and three windows. She had clear views of the hills, the woods and the castle, with its tower, locked up for good. Green paint blotted the walls. Books Leonardo published were balanced in piles and a framed poster of his bestseller hung above the bed.

She took a painting of a woman off the wall because she knew it would play night tricks on her. Anything with a face is dangerous. She was afraid of the dark.

People didn't scare her but seeing people that don't exist did. She let herself indulge in the occult only when it fit in a box of cards or a Tweet about the stars.

On the desk, which faced the woods' window, she placed the eyeball Leo the Rat gave her, and her old copy of *Hollywood Babylon*. She unpacked her suitcase and folded the clothes on the couch. Had she known the luggage meant for one week in New York would end up becoming her whole wardrobe, maybe she would have packed more thoughtfully. But you can't plan for disaster, can you. At least she had her tracksuit.

In the sink she splashed her face with cold water and stared at herself in the mirror. Her frown line fought for its life. On the airplane full of Europeans with regular faces, she decided to stop getting shots. Living where she did had warped her brain, made injections feel like groceries. If she ever went back to LA, she'd be an outlaw, a glitch in the system, both morally superior and physically uglier than those around her.

At some point in life, you have to accept decay. "Don't go crazy here." She plead with her reflection. "We're here to heal." This retreat would be her exile, jail, rehab, where she'd read, get ripped, and channel Balkan stoicism. Surely, she'd inherited it, she just had to find it. Her great-grandmother lived alone on the top of a mountain, with a goat, for fuckssake.

Dreaming the first night, she felt a warm touch on her throat. It wasn't a hand, not a solid, but something between air and liquid. A hot blob. Startled, she woke, paralyzed. Terrified of the blob, unable to brush it off, she struggled to open her eyes. Meanwhile she could hear herself panic. Her snores were fast and frightful. A wave of dread washed over her. The torture lasted an unclear, unbearable amount of time. Once she gained the ability to move, after she slapped her neck with her hand as if she were shooing off spiders, she turned on all the lights and consulted Google. Sleep paralysis was the scientific explanation, but the touch on her neck felt real. The sick sense lingered all day.

The following nights, to escape darkness, she slept at sunset and woke at dawn.

When she'd hear a black noise and feel panic, she'd calm down by thinking: why are ghosts only found in old castles, like this one? Why are ghosts always presumed rich? Why don't ghosts haunt bar bathrooms or broken-down cars? Maybe the afterlife is yet another luxury only promised to the wealthy. When she woke to find she made it through another night, she'd celebrate, running to the windows and flinging them open, the day dying to be loved.

As the sun unshadowed her walls she'd stretch, do push-ups, make the bed, brush her teeth and get dressed. Then she'd walk in the forest. Little birds cheered her on, their songs recalling past coke comedowns. The anxiety! She felt grateful not to be waiting on an Uber in an unknown neighborhood with a clogged nose, needing to eat and shit urgently. The desire to pick handfuls of wildflowers was overwhelming but she let them live. A couple of tree frogs were always together, stuck on top of each other, hopping over each other's heads.

A dirt road led her to the village, where she went only for groceries. The locals, misplaced from another century, looked at her funny. The ones she interacted with for food-purchasing purposes demanded to know why she inconvenienced them with her presence. "You aren't from here," they accused. Her solitude, at first sore, became its own balm. There was no Wi-Fi in her room and she didn't miss it. Words spilled from her and filled pages. The writing felt inevitable, like stepping into a puddle. She avoided the villa always, aside from mornings, when she'd climb the stone stairs past the pool, into the courtyard and through big, wooden doors, to the kitchen. She'd make herself a pot of coffee and rush it back to her room. She didn't need to cook food.

A construction worker came by some days of the week to fix a wall. A real "muratore," in cement-crusted overalls. His gray hair matched the dust. One morning, he knocked on her door and she opened it in her underwear. He said, "I brought you a croissant." It was delicious, though she wondered if by eating it she'd agreed to an intrusive, uncomfortable friendship. What's scarier, a ghost or a man? A man who knows you're in the middle of nowhere, all alone, without a car. He had a white van, upper-body strength, hammers and shovels. What could she do if things got vicious, hit him over the head with her laptop? Oh, but she did love pastries, especially when they're free... He spoke to her slowly, in careful, broken English, about the weather and the strays that ate from the tuna cans she left outside.

He told her the story about the woman who locked herself in that tower by her window and waited to die, then asked if she was scared to sleep there alone, and she lied. She didn't want him getting any heroic ideas.

Aside from the morally compromising croissants, her diet was yogurt and pickles for breakfast, canned vegetables for lunch and sandwiches for dinner. Cold, easy, military meals you can put together with some silverware. Skills she perfected back at the Beverly Motor Motel when she first moved to LA. On some unknown day, she'd lost count, she was shoveling peas smothered in Tabasco sauce into her mouth. Chewing serenely, she gazed over her laptop, out the window, into the woods, and that's when she saw.

ACKNOWLEDGMENTS

This story was inspired by Giancarlo DiTrapano and his legacy. Thanks to the DiTrapano foundation for letting me finish the manuscript in their haunted villa. Catherine and Giuseppe, grazie. My great friend and brilliant author, Allie Rowbottom. Christoph Paul and Maria Whelan, thanks for always "getting it." Alex Schubert, your art made this all come together. Thanks to Zagreb and to heartbreak. Hvala Mama, gracias Winkle.

ABOUT THE AUTHOR

Photo by Eric Scaggiante

Tea Hačić-Vlahović is a Croatian-American author. She's a columnist for *Vogue Adria* and *Spike Art Magazine*, host of *Troie Radicali* podcast and author of *Life of the Party* and *A Cigarette Lit Backwards*.

ALSO BY CLASH BOOKS

LIFE OF THE PARTY

Tea Hačić-Vlahović

HOW TO GET ALONG WITHOUT ME

Kate Axelrod

EARTH ANGEL

Madeline Cash

THREE WALLED WORLD

Ellery Capshaw

ALL OUR TOMORROWS

Amy DeBellis

AEMRICAN THIGHS

Elizabeth Ellen

GAG REFLEX

Elle Nash

MULHOLLAND DIVE

Vanessa Roveto

LOVER GIRL

Nicole Sellew

I CAN FIX HER

Rae Wilde